Love was never Mine...

Kunal Bhardwaj

Cedar books

Published by:

Cedar books

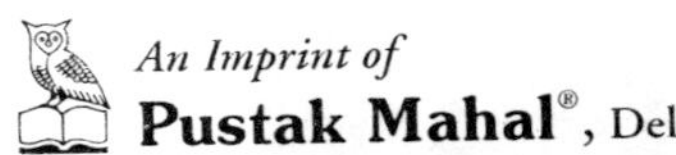

An Imprint of

Pustak Mahal®, Delhi

Administrative office and sale centre

J-3/16 , Daryaganj, New Delhi-110002

☎ 23276539, 23272783, 23272784 • *Fax:* 011-23260518

E-mail: info@pustakmahal.com • *Website:* www.pustakmahal.com

Branches

Bengaluru: ☎ 080-22234025 • *Telefax:* 080-22240209

E-mail: pustakmahalblr@gmail.com

Mumbai: ☎ 022-22010941, 022-22053387

E-mail: rapidex@bom5.vsnl.net.in

Patna: ☎ 0612-3294193 • *Telefax:* 0612-2302719

E-mail: rapidexptn@rediffmail.com

ISBN 978-81-223-1184-6

Edition 2015

Printed at : Radha Offset, Delhi

Dedicated to

My parents: They have always given me their support unconditionally.

My family: The love and bonding within such a large family is my inspiration.

The special person: Without whose presence, there would have been no inspiration for me to turn into a writer all of a sudden.

Acknowledgements

Whenever we do something extremely good or bad in life, it is a cumulative outcome of the support and critics provided by a lot of people whose names remain unknown. Therefore, I dedicate this page to thank all such people who gave their support and helped me out to make my novel turn into a reality. I would like to thank:

My family – I received each and every possible support I required, from my parents, grandparents, uncles, and aunt; whenever I needed them. I could not have got a better family than this one and sincerely thank God for the same.

My sister, and cousins – My sister Parul and my younger cousins (Prachi, Prerna, Shambhavi, Astha, Shrey, Dharita, Prateek, Shalini, Shiwani, Nishant, Somesh), who were great stress buster whenever I felt bored after a long session of writing. I used to spend time with them and feel myself re-energised again. I feel myself as the luckiest brother on earth.

Parul – One of the best friends of mine, who listened to me patiently whenever I needed (because I gave her no choice); and helped me shape this novel by providing constructive feedbacks.

Jyotsna, Kisha, Vishal, Ishani, Abhishek, Minakshi, Diwesh – My friends who provided their constructive feedback at times, and gave me all the support whenever I required.

Prasun, Gopi, Shashank, Abhishek – My best buddies, from whom I have learned one thing "Never Ever Look

Back, But Always Look Ahead". They are my pillars of self-confidence.

Genpact – I could not have got a better firm than this to work with, where I got each and every support I required turning my dreams into a reality. I was overwhelmed by their support to develop the creative part of their employees. The beautifully carved out cover page is a testimony of their efforts. I would like to especially thank Rachna and Raghu for patiently tolerating my repetitive buzzes and mails, and helping me out.

The Writing Lab – The guys did a fabulous job in editing. I guess I could not have got any better people than them to get the editing work done. Their understanding of words and emotions is impeccable.

Cedar Books, Pustak Mahal – For providing me a chance to get my story published to the world, and providing their kind support.

My friends on Facebook – I have bugged you all by continuously posting excerpts of my novel. But this was just a way to know the view of you people, as you all are the best judge. Also thanks to each one of you for providing your valuable comments time to time on each of my posts.

Romita, Arpita, Parivartan, Kavita, Manisha, and Vandana – For letting me understand the feelings of love blossoming inside.

AND LASTLY, Thanks to the one special person who taught me the meaning of love and its indispensability from understanding…

✧✧

Preface

I often used to watch movies and be happy about the heroes and heroines hating each other initially, then falling in love, and fighting with the villains for their love and winning the odd battle at last. Little did I know that most often than not, the person you love; you hardly get the love of the same person back to you.

We all have – some or the other time – regretted that had I accepted the love of that odd person, life would have been different. But the point remains how often we end up realising the right person's love at the right time.

Twenty years back, when I did not even know about the word love, let alone its meaning, I fell in love for the first time. Since then this most beautiful feeling in the world has struck me several times, and each time I felt myself portraying the character of Raj Kapoor in *Mera Naam Joker*.

I saw this movie first time when I was eight years old, and found it just an okay movie; even a bit lengthy. Saw the movie again when I was sixteen, and was able to connect with the mentality of a teenager who wants to live his own dreams. Then came age twenty-two, when I watched it for the third time and realised the maturity of Raj Kapoor's thoughts and the underlying pain which he went through; which was portrayed in the movie artistically.

It's only then when I decided to pay a tribute to this eternal movie through my own novel, and my endless journey thus begun with a new meaning thereafter.

This book not only discloses the inner layers of human emotions, but also exposes those several smaller moments when our soft feelings get crushed unknowingly; but such moments remain unsaid, unexposed because the moments are very small. Remember only such moments or incidents are small, not their impact or outcome.

I remember one such incident. Once an old friend of mine called me up after a very long time saying that it's been a long gap and she would like to have dinner with me at some XYZ restaurant. Hearing this, the whole day I was busy planning about the restaurant where we would go. I quickly finished my day's work and left home a bit early. Since I was meeting her after a long time, while returning I bought a gift which I knew she liked the most. After coming back home, the next hour was completely dedicated to plan for the dress I would be wearing. I was all set to leave, when I got a call from her that she is going somewhere else and we will meet up some other time. Now remember the incident from her point of view is very small, but the impact?? Well, only you all can decide.

This book is not just a book for me. For me, it's an effort to reunite the thing called "Love". It's a medium to express the hidden emotions and unsaid painful feelings to millions of lovers to make them understand the indispensability of love and understanding.

So all I can say is that though "Love Was never Mine..." for you all my effort is towards "Love was Always Ours...."

Prologue

Shreya's reactions were numbed. She didn't say a word and involuntarily widened the door for the men to come in and keep the body. She kept staring at them while they kept the body in the centre of her drawing room.

"Madam, everything will be alright," a man came close to her and tried to give her solace. She couldn't hear a word.

"A car hit him. We were working nearby. He was hit badly," another one of the men said, in broken English and continued, "we took him to the hospital in an auto rickshaw, but he was already dead. The doctor found out his wallet from his jeans which had the address of here."

She didn't look at him as he spoke. It was as though he was speaking some foreign language that was incomprehensible to her. She quietly gazed at the body lying in front of her and wondered when it might jump at her. It didn't.

"We noted the car number which hit him. He was driving at a very fast speed. Here, this is the car's number," a man in a vest and a thin cloth wrapped around his legs spoke and gave her a white chit which had some digits and alphabets written on it.

BN 01 F 5678. It was gibberish to her. She couldn't comprehend the shape and the structure of the writing on the paper. The men quietly went away, without saying another word. And she was left all to herself, except the white chit of paper and her husband's body. She stared at the paper in her left hand again to make sense of what was happening.

And a feeling of outrageousness ran through her. Her subconscious mind told her it was a number she had come across and then it dawned on her – it was the number of Rahul's car. Her grief turned into extreme anger and without a second thought, she got up, took the car keys hanging near the entrance as usual and stomped towards her car. She forgot about her husband's body lying inside the house; she forgot she had to call up her and her husband's family to inform them about the incident; she forgot everything about her social obligations and duties. All she wanted was revenge for the act and harming Rahul was the only plausible way she could think of.

She didn't feel any emotions inside her, except that of anger and betrayal. Her soul didn't say a word, as if it has vanished altogether. She drove the car at a breakneck speed, without paying any heed to the traffic rules. It was six in the morning and there wasn't much traffic around.

Hardly putting the foot on the brake, she honked the way through the streets. The car was going at full throttle, and something strange happened all of a sudden.

While driving she heard someone calling out her name, so slowly as if it's coming from the far end of a dark tunnel. She looked around to find out the person but all she could see in front was heavy fog. It seemed as if someone is slowly taking control over her and trying to invade her thoughts.

Never before had she felt so scared. She was already sweating profusely, and the car's steering was wet. Her mind went blank for a moment, and she felt as if someone is playing a movie right in front of her eyes...

The Meeting

A black sedan screeched to a halt outside the swanky gates of Hewlett-Packard. At the wheel was Shrey, who had come to drop his cousin, Rahul. Dressed in a crisp white shirt – ironed to perfection, striped blue tie – with a perfect dimpled knot, fitted grey trousers – falling immaculately on his silhouette, well polished shoes, a leather belt, hair neatly combed, Rahul looked every bit a fresher.

It was his first day at the job; a new chapter in his life, a chapter which would define the rest of his journey. Stepping out from the car, he couldn't help but grin at the quirky, red and green colour of the office's facade. *An unpeeled watermelon*, he thought, chuckling at his own weird imagination.

Rahul was a quintessential guy-next-door whose only ambition in life was to work for an MNC and earn big bucks. With his average looks, a lanky frame and a slightly diffident manner, he knew he could only fit into a nine-to-five schedule. A warm smile and an affectionate personality were the only weapons he had when it came to winning friends; and he didn't have many.

Back in college, he couldn't be called a bookworm but was nevertheless a diligent guy who always attended his lectures and listened to his professors – something that was considered an exception rather than a rule in college. He worked hard not because he liked studying; he worked hard just to fulfil his dream of working in a corporate firm. And that dream was standing right in front of him.

The imposing gates of the building looked like a huge milestone to him, a milestone he was about to achieve. This feeling of achievement made him anxious and elated at the same time. His throat ran dry with nervous excitement. He was going through the same emotions a tiny-tot goes through on the first day of school; a teenager goes through on the first day in a new city; a lover goes through before proposing his love.

Tightening the noose of his tie and smoothening out the nonexistent wrinkles from the shirt, he gripped his documents closer to his side and took small, seminal steps towards the red and green structure.

This is my big ticket. After all those years of hard work, finally I will be able to earn a living for myself. Finally, I can make my own decisions, he thought, trying to break away from the nervous thoughts that were plaguing his mind since the night before.

He had turned and twisted in bed all night long, unable to sleep, imagining every possible situation that could happen to him on the first day at office.

Look at that nerd. He wouldn't be able to survive here even for a week. Laughter! Wow, prim and proper. What is he thinking of himself – the CEO of this company? More laughter! Why can't you do such a simple task? What have you done in college? Freshers are such a pain in the ass!

A remark from one end and some sarcasm from the other was all he could imagine while lying in bed.

As he approached the doors of the office, made from translucent glass and bearing a huge logo of Hewlett-Packard in green, the weight of the glass seemed two-fold to him under the weight of his negative emotions. He could have easily buckled down under his own weight had it not been for a silent prayer he kept repeating to himself, asking for strength from the Almighty, until he reached the first floor of the building. As he turned right from the staircase, he saw the wooden doors which were his ticket to a lifetime of happiness and enjoyment.

Three normal steps were all that was needed to get to the doors; it took him eight. Standing in front of the wooden doors, he caught his breath, took a good look at himself one last time and finally pushed the doors open. A cool draft of air rushed from inside. The coolness of the air from the air conditioner and his own anxiety made his stomach churn.

Wow! First day of my corporate life and straight into the conference room, he said to himself, sarcastically. As if his own nervousness was not enough, fifty pairs of eyes shot up all at once, as he stepped inside the dimly lit conference room. The attention made him even more self-conscious. Never been subjected to such a situation before, he fumbled with words and all he could come up with was – "May I come in?"

"You are already in," retorted a voice from the other end of the room. His sweaty palms let go off the heavy wooden door completely, which he was holding onerously until then, resulting in a huge thud.

Desperate to get away from the attention, he glanced up and down the length of the conference room for a vacant chair, but there was none. The plush interiors, the dim lighting, the attention, the search for the chair … everything added up to make his first moment of corporate life a rather messy one. The beads of sweat were now visible on his forehead.

He quickly settled down on the edge of the window, the only vacant spot in the room. He wished he could jump out of that window right away, onto the street and away from the cool interiors and cold people of the room. He wished he could go out in the sun, feel the warmth right down to his bones, feel free again, until he heard the voice that changed his mind.

"Could you please pass on the attendance sheet?" asked a voice from the far end of the conference table. Glancing up, Rahul saw a pleasant face asking him to pass on the sheet of paper lying by his side. Those eight matter-of-factly words evoked a strange feeling in him, a feeling of connection; and the picture in front of his eyes left him mesmerised.

Long auburn hair carefully tied into a ponytail; big, inquisitive eyes having a certain kind of amiability to them; a face so radiant, one could see every contour of it even in the dim interiors. Something tingled inside him as he tried hard to divert his attention from the nude, slightly parted pink lips; their movement took him on a roller coaster ride – his heart skipping a beat with every word that came out from the motion of the tender lines.

It took a few moments before he came back to his senses and finally, he was able to comprehend the sweet sounding frequency which had transported him to his own wonderland.

"Excuse me, could you please pass on the attendance sheet?" quipped the voice a third time. Fumbling with pen in the hand and a multitude of thoughts in his head, he picked up the sheet and walked towards the girl dressed in a pink sleeveless top and a pencil skirt. The pen dropped twice from his hand before the sheet reached her extended arm.

Rahul's hand brushed hers as he gave the sheet to her and his intestines convulsed at that warm, soft touch. Gingerly, he made the walk back to his spot by the window, half conscious that he was in the conference room of a company he had joined barely half an hour back.

The orientation program commenced with a keynote speech by the manager of the marketing department, followed by the company's goals, growth and all the jargon one associates with business meetings and trainings. Rahul was oblivious to it all. All he did during the eight hours of the orientation program was steal a glance every minute of the gorgeous face he had unexpectedly come across, who was now sitting with folded hands and an erect posture, at the far right corner of the conference table.

Back home, he could hardly remember a word that the trainer had said. All he could gather from the orientation session was her voice, her silky touch, her petite contours, her confident manner and the warmth that she radiated.

Not a bad day at all, he thought, as he lay in bed that night, wide awake, finding it hard to let go of her thoughts. His mind kept wandering to her soft pink lips, the way she spoke, the way she carried herself. He was spellbound by her beauty like a snake to a snake charmer's rhythm.

The next morning, he was up early, feeling more energetic than ever before. He was eagerly looking forward to the day; to an encounter with her mesmerising spell again. He desperately wanted her to cast him in her spell – everyday, every minute and every second. He was as excited as a homeless kid who has just found a tiny hut to live in. In this frenzy, he changed his clothes almost a dozen times.

This pink shirt looks really cool! I am sure she would notice me in this. Standing in front of a full length mirror, with the shirt properly buttoned and tucked into his pleated grey trousers, he took a good look at himself from every angle imaginable. A little walk towards the mirror; a side pose with hands crossed in front of his chest; another side pose from the other angle, this time with his hands in his pockets; a little walk backwards. *No, this looks a little girlish. I should wear something more macho, more masculine. Girls love macho guys.*

With the freshly ironed pink shirt on the floor, it was time for the blue one to pass the test. Again, the same routine was followed – a little walk towards the mirror, a few side poses, a little walk backwards and the blue one also found the same fate as the pink. This routine continued for a good one hour before he was finally able to decide on a striped mauve shirt; pleated grey trousers; black shoes so shiny that he would not need a mirror the entire day; cufflinks he had bought five years ago and had worn only on special occasions and the original leather belt he had worn the day before.

Satisfied with the way he was looking, he poured an entire bottle of a not-so-nice perfume (because that was all he had), locked the door of his flat carefully and left for his second day at the office. Hari, his childhood friend, who worked in the same office, was waiting outside in his car, trying to control his raging anger for Rahul's unusual dress rehearsals.

Hari was a well built guy with dark bushy eyebrows which almost got lost in the background of his dark complexion. He had curly, short cropped hair, an average height, less than average looks but a splendid taste for women. Calling Hari a nymphomaniac was an understatement. And ironically, he was still a virgin, just like Rahul.

But Rahul's virginity was a matter of choice. He valued emotions more than the physical aspect of things and that was always evident in the way he treated those inferior to him. He had the kind of humbleness one would associate with an ascetic – with someone who does not derive pleasure from materialistic things. Rahul always wanted true love and he had not found it so far, until he came across the enchanting beauty of a girl on the first day of his corporate life; a girl he had seen just once and not even spoken to. He was sure it was true love because he had never felt the way he was feeling now – giddy from the thoughts of seeing her again.

On the other hand, Hari was a virgin by circumstances. He did not care a hoot about love and relationships. All he wanted was raw sex; and unfortunately, he had never got the opportunity to fulfil the fantasies he built while watching hardcore XXX action. He could have made love to a donkey with breasts if only he got the chance. Hari too cared for people's emotions but only if they were friends. He was the typical guy who was wary of the C word and was ever ready to get into a no strings attached relationship.

While on their way to office, Rahul felt the urge to discuss his new found feelings with Hari but restrained from doing so, lest he be made the butt of his jokes. Instead, they chatted about the usual – new gadgets launched, the latest hottie to hit the silver screen, their future plans ... Rahul only partially listening to what Hari was blabbering, his mind wandering off time and again to the prospect of feeling her warmth again.

They reached office twenty minutes before their training was to start and barged straight into the conference room. Expectedly enough, they were the first ones to arrive. Rahul desperately looked around for her presence, his eyes scanning the conference room repeatedly, although his mind had already told him she had not arrived. His heart was thumping, nearly audibly, in anticipation of her aroma filling the conference room any moment.

As there was still time for the training to start, Hari decided to go downstairs for a fag as the employees were not allowed to smoke inside the office premises. Rahul was not a smoker but tagged along just so that he could see her before anybody else does in office. The thought of other guys checking her out made him cringe in disgust. *They do not deserve her. All they look at is her physical beauty. None of them have ever realised how beautiful her soul is. Her soul is mine, she is mine*, he said to himself, as they were waiting for the lift to arrive.

In his desperation, Rahul kept pushing the lift button until the doors finally opened. And immediately, Rahul was transported to his wonderland. There she was, dressed in black, from head to toe. Stepping out from the elevator, she walked past the guys, ignorant of their presence and towards the training room. *She did not even notice me*, Rahul thought dejected that the mauve he was wearing came a cropper. *But she does not even know me. Why would she look at me?* He thought again, trying to pep up his sagging spirit.

With a quick pat on Hari's back, he ran down the corridor, following her sensuous fragrance; her tiptoeing footsteps – that were echoing through the hallway; her magnetism that she was unaware of.

Both of them entered the conference room together and others soon followed suit, much to Rahul's dismay. He had hoped he would get the chance to spend a few moments alone with her presence. He had hoped he would get to admire her grace, her aura without the presence of other pairs of eyes.

But sadly, it was almost training time and the trainees started settling down in their seats, taking away Rahul's few moments of solitude with her existence.

As the people were still settling down, the trainer entered the room and Hari just managed to scrape in before she closed the doors. The trainer was a woman in her late thirties, with a stern expression on her face and a manner of speaking which immediately put her pupils to attention, albeit superficially.

Hari took the chair next to Rahul, whispering in his ear simultaneously as he settled down –"So you have the hots for Shreya huh? You bastard!"

"Who Shreya?" Rahul asked, genuinely perplexed at his remark.

"The girl in black; who you just followed asshole!"

"Oh, ok. What hots? She is a nice girl but —", Rahul paused, searching for words.

"But what? You like her, right?"

"Yes."

"And so do most of the guys here."

The last matter-of-factly statement by Hari made Rahul clinch his fist on impulse. Rahul was surprised at his own reaction. He was a very soft-spoken guy who never picked up a fight with anybody, no matter what the situation. But that last sentence that Hari spoke evoked feelings in him that he himself was unaware of.

He despised the fact that people are so obsessed with the physical aspect of things. He wanted to change them all; he wanted to guide them to something deeper than superficial outer appearance. *Why can't people see the beauty of the soul? Why can't they see beyond the outer form?*

He did not hate people who are obsessed with physicality. But he hated the whole idea of a physical connection sans an emotional connect. Little did he know what was in store for him.

Sitting a good distance away from Shreya, he could still catch her every breath. Throughout the training, he kept thinking about ways to initiate a conversation with her. The boring lecture being meted out by the trainer didn't help matters a great deal. *How do I talk to her? What should I say to her?* That is what he kept thinking about and suddenly, he remembered a phrase he had read sometime back in a novel – "When you aspire for something wholeheartedly, you are bound to get it". He totally believed in it. He always wanted to enter the corporate field and he did. And he was sure he would get Shreya, because he really wanted her.

Pepped up with this new found belief, he was feeling more confident of himself but still, that elusive question evaded him – *How do I talk to her?*

And while he was struggling with the question, the trainer announced a forty-five minute break for all, much to his relief. *Thank you!* he exclaimed, looking upwards, thankful that he finally got the chance to get away from the soporific lecture and more importantly, her enchanting presence.

He could now get his thoughts in order and think of a way to start a conversation with her. He quickly folded his training schedule, put it in the left pocket of his trousers and strolled his way with Hari downstairs to grab a bite. And unknowingly, he followed her.

Maybe the universe wants me to talk to her right now, he thought. *When you aspire for something wholeheartedly, you definitely get it.* The thought reverberated in his head as he made his way to the food stall outside the office along with Hari. She was already there, waiting to place her order.

The food stall was Hari's favourite hangout zone, something which was starting to reflect in his protruding belly. Hari always savoured the buttered paratha along with the spicy mashed chickpea vegetable that was served as an accompaniment. And of course, the price was another factor which swung Hari's vote in favour of this popular Indian junk food over other stuff. One could have a complete plate of chickpea and paratha for a measly ten bucks.

Having been born and brought up in a money conscious family, Hari's choice of food was not surprising at all to Rahul.

Rahul promptly ordered two for himself and four for Hari, without even consulting him. *Okay, it is now or never. I have got to speak to her*, Rahul told himself, determined to break the ice with Shreya but shaking at the thought of it.

With bated breath and a pounding heartbeat, he approached Shreya, still not sure how to get a conversation started.

"Excuse me," he said, half expecting a no response from her. But to his surprise, and his nervous delight, she turned instantly, with her big, beautiful eyes staring right at him, waiting for him to go on.

Standing with an erect posture, arms dropped casually by her side, shoulders pegged back only slightly in a confident manner which was not arrogant, lips firmly pursed together – she was so close to Rahul that the slightest of movements by either of them in the right direction would have resulted in more than a brush of their clothing. And this propinquity to her gave him goose bumps.

"Er ... may I talk to you for a moment?" was all he could muster with a stutter.

"Hmm, yea sure," came back the reply which did not have the slightest of the puzzled tone which one would associate with such an encounter. Shreya was used to such attention from the opposite sex, and she enjoyed it to a certain degree.

Unsure of what to say next, he sensed his valiant effort of making the first move going in vain; until the universe intervened.

A girl in a casual green t-shirt and blue, bell-bottomed jeans tapped Shreya on her shoulder with an effervescent greeting. It was Riya, Rahul's school time friend. "Hi Shreya, How are you?"

"Hey Riya, I am fantastic. You tell me, how are you?"

"I am good too. Wow, we have a lot to catch up on."

Riya was a girl full of life. She had the kind of enthusiasm about life usually associated with a toddler who has just learnt to walk. Her bubbly nature always rubbed off on other people and that's what Rahul loved about her. Riya was nowhere as beautiful as Shreya but still, her positive and devil-may-care attitude attracted a lot of male attention; Rahul wasn't ever attracted to her though. Rahul and Riya were the sort of friends who could roll over each other in bed without feeling even the slightest of physical intimacy. There didn't exist even a semblance of intimate attraction between them which one would associate between opposite genders.

The two girls started chatting like they were long lost buddies, completely ignoring the presence of Rahul.

What is it with girls? How can they talk nonstop? Where do they get their energy from? We sure can benefit a lot from their source of energy. There would definitely be lesser fights and lesser breakups if only we could get hold of that source, he thought, amused at the behaviour of the two chirping figures in front of him; yet, silently relieved that Riya intervened, giving him a breathing space. He knew if it was not for Riya, he would have made a fool of himself.

The girls just could not stop talking. Rahul stood there as a mere spectator, watching the spectacle of his best friend and his first love engaged in a conversation like there was no tomorrow. It was the first time he was seeing Shreya so animated; the vibrant energy of the moment made him restless. He was silently praying that Riya introduce him to Shreya; and his prayer was answered.

After about ten minutes of passionate chatting with her girl pal, Riya finally noticed the presence of Rahul, who was standing barely a foot away from Shreya, making a pathetic attempt at looking disinterested.

"Hey dodo, what are you doing there standing like an ass?" Riya said, in her usual, lighthearted and lively manner. Rahul and Riya always poked fun at each other. When in each other's company, they always behaved like kids left alone in a candy store – cheerful and vivacious.

"You didn't even call me after landing up a job. Not fair," Riya continued trying to sound miffed with Rahul.

"Anyways, meet my friend Shreya. Shreya, this is Rahul, my school time buddy and my best friend," she said, looking first at Rahul and then at Shreya, waiting for them to shake hands.

If you want something wholeheartedly, the whole universe conspires to get it for you. Rahul's belief in the universe just got stronger with that introduction to Shreya. "Hi", said Shreya, her arm outstretched, waiting for Rahul to shake hands. He could not believe his luck. The same soft hands he had a brush with on his first day in office were now waiting for his grip. He had to try hard to behave normally.

"Hi," he replied, shaking hands with her gently, with a broad grin on his face. He tried his best to conceal his fidgetiness but failed at it miserably. His eyes were blinking more than usual, he was constantly shifting his weight from one leg to another, trying to find a comfortable standing position and he was trying hard to look into those beautiful eyes but couldn't keep his eyes there long enough.

Shreya sensed his uneasiness and a smile broke across her face, seeing a guy who was so bashful of meeting a girl. Little did she know that the shy guy who was standing in front of her, trying desperately to find some words, was in love with her.

Never sure of his communication skills, Rahul thought it best to divert his attention to the parathas.

"What will you have Riya?" he asked, unintentionally speaking louder than usual.

"I will have a *Gobi* paratha and an *Aloo* paratha," she replied, perplexed at his unusual behaviour.

What has happened to him? No kiddish behaviour, no fighting for a treat. Why is he acting so gentlemanly, so sophisticated? Riya thought, trying to decode his behaviour.

Amidst all this, Hari was busy gorging on his hot parathas, oblivious to the presence of the other three. When it came to food that was cheap and tasty at the same time, nothing mattered to him. He could have spent the whole day at the food stall, had somebody agreed to pay for his bill.

"What will you have Shreya?" Rahul asked, in a soft tone.

"I'll just have a *Gobi* paratha, without butter," she replied, hesitantly, with a smile on her face.

"Without butter? Health conscious or on a diet?" he said, glad that he finally got something to say to her.

Shreya just stood there smiling, without giving a reply.

Rahul promptly placed the order for the girls, shouting at the vendor to get his voice heard among the swarm.

The three of them engaged in some casual chit chat while their order was being prepared. Most of the conversation was dominated by Riya's grudges against Rahul – the fact that he hadn't called up for so long; the fact that he hadn't informed her about his job. But Riya didn't get too much chance to scold him, as their order arrived early.

Standing by the side, finding it hard to balance the hot plates in their hands, all of them, nevertheless, enjoyed the parathas; everybody, except Rahul. He was so busy seeing Shreya having small bites of her unbuttered paratha with her tender hands, he forgot to savour his own.

And in stark contrast to Rahul was Hari, who, after enjoying seven scrumptious parathas, was busy arguing with the vendor for selling them at such an exorbitant cost of Rs 12; not that he was paying for his share of parathas; that was as usual paid by Rahul.

Rahul paid for all four of them and it was time to go back to the boring training session. Dodging their way through the milling crowd and the remnants of the sludge from the overnight rain, Hari, Rahul and Shreya bid adieu to Riya and made their way to the conference room.

"Rahul, your twelve bucks," said Shreya, as she tried returning him the amount.

"Oh come on! I'm not taking that. It's such a small amount. Don't worry. Chill," came back the reply, as he tried resisting her putting the amount in his pocket. The resistance resulted in their bodies coming in contact with each other, with Rahul almost clutching her hands to avoid the ten rupee note and the two rupee coin from going into his pocket. He was not enjoying the drama over a meagre amount of twelve bucks but he was definitely enjoying the opportunity he was getting to hold her hand, which allowed him to feel and absorb the warmth of her body and that of her soul.

"Okay. I would not return them only on one condition," said Shreya.

"And what is that condition?"

"Next time, I am treating you for lunch. Fine?"

"Okay," said Rahul, with a hint of smile across his lips. He wasn't going to say no to an opportunity to have lunch with her. The introduction to Shreya, the grip of her supple skin and the invitation for a lunch with her truly made his day and the training session was a breeze after that. He spent the entire session with the thoughts of the brief encounter with Shreya and in anticipation of the brief encounter turning into a lifetime of togetherness with her.

Everything around him suddenly appeared more beautiful to him; on his way back home with Hari, he was the one who was blabbering about anything and everything; his excitement was palpable and Hari took full advantage of it.

"So, you finally got to hold her hand. Good going sir," said Hari, indulging in some good humoured mockery with him.

"Piss off. Why are you sounding so jealous?"

"Me? Jealous? Why should I be jealous? I do not have the hots for her, although she is a nice chick, no doubt," said Hari, with a snigger, 'coz he knew Rahul could not tolerate sexually indicative remarks against her.

Rahul understood his intentions and played along with him, their banter continuing throughout their one and a half hour journey on the potholed roads, until Hari dropped Rahul at his place.

The excitement of the day gone by and the anticipation of the day about to arrive left Rahul turning and tossing in bed yet again. The next morning, he got up early, excitedly looking forward to the day, like a struggler eagerly looking forward to his first release.

Things Move Forward

He was to be inducted in the group, and despite the unknown element attached to the induction, he was, to his own surprise, not nervous at all. With the new found zest for living, he got ready for office, expectant of breaking into her sensual aura again.

As was the routine, Hari picked him up from his place and they both reached office half an hour before the reporting time. But they didn't have much time to kill as the HR person arrived soon after. She was a woman in her late twenties, with striking facial features and a hurried gait.

"Isn't she hot?" said Hari, making lecherous gestures behind her back as she guided them through a hallway to a small cabin with a semitransparent glass door.

A woman, with long, dark brown hair, big eyelashes, a slightly dusky complexion and full lips which were further enhanced by a dark pink shade of lipstick, was sitting behind a square wooden table, comfortably perched on a plush leather chair.

"Hi, I am Varsha, your project manager," she said, as she stood up from her cross-legged position, shaking hands with each of them in turn.

"Come along, I will show you your seat. Your team members haven't come as yet. I will introduce them to you later in the day," she said to Rahul, as she opened the cabin door, waiting for them to follow.

She took a slight left and walked through another corridor – this time a slightly wider one than the last that Hari and Rahul had traversed.

Hari's eyes lit up seeing her swaying gait and her powerful persona. He always fantasised about going to bed with a domineering woman and watching Varsha, he couldn't help but imagine getting into every possible sexual position described in the revered Kamasutra with her.

After two-three minutes of walking on the gray marble floor of the hospital like corridor, Varsha stopped before a completely transparent door made of heavy glass. Rahul could see the view inside. It was a large hall with about a hundred desktops and at small distances from each other on wooden tables which were joined together to form a complete row. As far as he could see, there were about ten such rows, each of equal length.

Varsha touched the plastic card dangling from a strap around her neck on the small white board to the right of the glass door. There was a tiny beep accompanied by the sound of a click synonymous with the opening of locks. She pushed open the door and walked straight to the second bay.

"This will be your seat Rahul," she said, as she indicated to the fourth chair from the starting of the bay, facing the door.

"And that shall be your seat Hari," she said, pointing to the seat two places right to that of Rahul, before she disappeared from the hall, tiptoeing gracefully, much to Hari's delight.

Rahul sat down on the orange chair, which was like the rest of them in the hall – four legged, with wheels underneath and armrests on either side. The height of the chair was not comfortable for him and he had to fight a little with the long knob underneath the seat of the chair to adjust its height to his comfort level.

Although it was almost reporting time, there were only ten others apart from Rahul and Hari; and none of them seemed to be interested in work. A guy to the far left of Rahul was viewing some racy wallpaper of the latest Hollywood chicks while the one in the immediate next bay was busy saving his Pinball from falling into space.

Their systems were yet to be configured, so they decided to spend their free time doing something constructive. Hari logged on to a soft porn website while Rahul decided to know more about the company via Google. He searched everything he could about the company – the founders, the founding year, the yearly turnover, the workforce, the global presence and everything else associated with a company that has been around for decades. He found immense satisfaction in the fact that he was the only one working there while the rest were whiling away their precious time. It made him feel proud and important.

But this feeling of pride did not last long. He had barely known enough about the company when people started arriving, followed by the din of drawers being opened, instructions being shouted and greetings being exchanged. After the gruelling two days of listening to boring lectures and going through tiresome training sessions in an environment where even the most introvert would get sick, he was glad to see some buzz around the place.

He had seen such a workplace atmosphere only in movies before and being a part of it in real life gave him a sense of accomplishment. On the other hand, Hari was dejected on seeing people arrive so early. He had to bid adieu to the naked breasts and the orgasmic expressions for the day.

Both of them got curious looks and some introductions, too, from the by-passers.

"Hi, freshers?" said a tall, bespectacled guy, quickly shaking hands with them before disappearing in his bay.

"Hello, good morning. I am Neha, from the administration department. I am responsible for giving you your identity cards and stuff. Do let me know if you have any issues", said a bony girl, before making to her seat.

The office was full of people, making their way between ways, with a sense of urgency and responsibility. Even the Pinball playing guy was busy solving a customer's query on the phone. There was a lot of activity around but still Rahul felt a sense of emptiness around him. He could see a lot of people moving around the place but not the soul he was looking for. Shreya had not yet arrived.

Where is she? Why is she so late? Has something happened to her? Oh God, I hope she is okay. She always came on time for the training. She must have got stuck in something really bad. All kinds of thoughts ran through his head, giving him anxious moments before he finally caught her glance.

Dressed in a pink shirt with three-fourth length sleeves, pleated black trousers and a stole around her neck, she made quick strides towards the exact same bay Rahul was sitting in, her handbag making frantic to and fro motions with each stride.

She had already had a chat over the phone with Miss Varsha, and she had told her about her designated seat. She approached her seat, which was to the right of Rahul's. Rahul felt as if he had been honoured with an Oscar, and his elation knew no bounds when he realised he would be sitting right next to the girl he was most probably in love with.

"Hi Rahul, how are you?" she said, as she extended her arm to shake hands with him.

"I am good," he said, trying hard to look as disinterested as possible.

"Hey Hari, what's up?" she said, waving her hand casually at Hari, who was desperately trying to close all the porn windows he had opened in the last half an hour.

"Hi," was all she got from the other end.

"Rahul, we barely know each other, which is why I feel a little embarrassed to ask for a small favour. Could you please help me out with something urgent I have been assigned by Miss Varsha?" she said.

"And what is that?" said Rahul, making a pathetic attempt at looking sombre. Even a blind man could have sensed his excitement at that point from the eager tone of his voice which completely defied his straight face expression.

" Actually…." she said, taking a deliberate pause, unsure of whether she should ask for such a favour from a guy she had just met a day ago. "It is Prerna's birthday today. Prerna is one of our team members," she continued, while she cracked her knuckle of her index finger to hide her indecisiveness.

"The rest of the team members are busy today and even my boyfriend is out of town. I do not have anybody who could help me with selecting a gift for her," she said, while she bit her lower lip ever so slightly, conscious of her every word.

She has a boyfriend. I do not have a chance with her, Rahul's brain screamed as he grappled with the new found truth.

"Can you please accompany me to the market? I find it really hard to select a gift for someone," she said, her head tilting to one side and her nude lips twirling up as she forced a smile in order to avoid coming across as pushy.

"Sure, no problem. But are you sure you want to take me along? Because I am not good at either," said Rahul, emphasising more than he desired on the 'me'.

"Hmmm, I am sure two brains would be better than one. We will leave around lunch time. Thank you so much."

"Okay," he said, giving his shoulders a casual shrug, as he got back to the computer screen.

She has a boyfriend. His heart sank with that thought. He stared blankly at the screen in front of him which had yellow smileys dancing all over it, as if rejoicing at the new revelation.

Why am I wasting my time with her when I know I do not stand a chance? He ruminated, trying to find a logical explanation to the affirmative answer he gave her a minute back. There came none.

If you want something wholeheartedly, the whole universe conspires to get it for you. The thought sprung up yet again in his contemplating psyche. It brought a faint smile on his face, as he continued to unravel his ambiguous feelings.

He was being torn apart by two contradictory forces within his soul – one that tried to comprehend the futility of going closer to her, and the other which tried to defy all logic and make him believe in the power of true love.

His mental ordeal was partially broken when a man, who looked to be in his early thirties, approached him from behind with a formal introduction.

"Hi, I am Gaurav. I am the systems engineer here and I will be configuring your computer for the e-mail and other stuff," he said, in his sonorous voice, as he quickly grabbed a vacant chair lying close by, seemingly not interested in any further formalities.

He frantically tapped a few keys until the screen changed from dancing smileys to pitch black, with a cursor blinking on the top left corner. A few gibberish commands were all that was needed for him to do the job.

"Your username is Rahul.Sharma and your password is Rahuls1. In case you have any problem, drop me a mail at Gaurav.baweja@hp.com," he said sans any emotions, hurriedly got up from the chair and went to Hari's desk where he repeated the same procedure.

Hari, who had diligently attended the training session, quickly got on with the job once his system was configured, as he was aware of the procedures to be followed and the tasks to be completed. Rahul was not. He had devoted his complete attention to Shreya during the training sessions, barring a few minutes in between when her presence overwhelmed his senses.

His lack of knowledge about the procedures and the cerebral confusion that he was undergoing at that moment made him uneasy and embarrassed.

"Shreya, could you please tell me the tasks to be done?" he said, with a sheepish expression, mortified at his own ignorance during the training.

Shreya, glued to her computer screen, quickly spat out a few mundane tasks to keep him busy. She was too occupied to bother about his ashamed expressions, and Rahul was thankful to God for that.

OOO

"Hey Rahul, let's go," Shreya said, as she picked up her own handbag and her car keys and made her way to the door.

It was lunchtime and they were supposed to go gift shopping for Prerna, their teammate. Rahul willingly obliged and followed her quick steps towards the exit.

"Thanks again for coming Rahul. I really, really appreciate it," she said obligingly, bending slightly from her hips which made her chest protrude towards him, while she squeezed her arms and tightened her shoulders, much the same way as a kid requesting profusely for an ice lolly.

"No, don't say that. It's my duty," Rahul replied, glad that his gesture had made her so happy. He no longer wondered why he was with her, his inner turmoil was no longer there; all he knew was he had made her happy and that was what mattered to him the most.

Rahul opened the door for her, eager to show his chivalrous side and they both made their way through the long hallway to the main exit door. It was slightly cloudy outside but they were not dark, rain bearing clouds. They stepped outside together and gave the same expressions, almost simultaneously.

Teeth grinded together, nose twitched up and eyes on the verge of closing – the typical human expression when suddenly subjected to high temperatures. The high humidity level was palpable and they felt the stickiness of the atmosphere even more, coming from an air conditioned environment.

Literally sprinting, Shreya quickly got into her black Skoda which was parked near the main gates, while Rahul casually strolled to the car and settled into the passenger seat. He found her childish behaviour amusing and lovable.

How could I even think of saying no to a chance of spending an entire evening with her? He thought, as he mulled over the confusions he had a while back. *I deserve a punishment for ignoring the universe's will. Punish me God, for doubting your prowess. Please punish me,* almost talking to his Universe, half expecting the Almighty to deliver him a blow then and there.

She put the key in ignition, promptly switched on the car's air conditioner and made her way out of the parking lot.

"Who is Prerna by the way? I haven't met her. In fact, I haven't met any of the team members," he said, eager to have a conversation with her. He didn't give a damn about who Prerna was and who all his team members were. He desperately wanted to show her that he is a confident guy who isn't shy of interacting with people.

"Even I don't know. The task has been handed over to me by the project manager. Let's see," she said, with a smile, while she kept her eyes firmly on the road.

That was the last sentence spoken by either of them in their half an hour journey until they reached the Archies gift shop. Rahul was content sitting so close to her and feeling the confidence and the magnetism that she exuded. He did not want to disturb the serenity of the moment by filling the air with his vocal vibrations.

She carefully parked the car by the side of the shop, took her handbag which she had kept on the backseat of the car and followed Rahul into the shop.

He had no idea what he was doing in a gift shop. He had never bought a gift for his parents or any of his friends, leave alone a person he had never seen. *That teddy bear looks nice. That clock looks good too. Those wind chimes are beautiful*….he thought, as he moved from one shelf to another, liking almost anything he saw. *How is it possible for somebody to choose from such a variety of items? Why at all do we give gifts?* Who started the tradition of giving gifts? Perplexed, he started regretting his decision of saying yes to gift shopping.

He didn't have a clue about gifts; nevertheless, he moved around the small but cluttered shop, feeling the many items on the way and then keeping them back with utmost care.

Shreya was walking just beside him, carefully scrutinising each and every item kept on the shelves, checking the price tag of items that she found suitable as a birthday gift. It was almost half an hour since they had entered the shop but none of them could find anything that they could give as a gift to their teammate.

"Did you find anything?" she said, matter-of-factly.

"There is such a lot here. I am confused."

"How is this for a gift?" she asked, picking up a small glass frame, which was in the shape of a book with a phrase written on it which read – "Success and failure is temporary. What matters the most is the drive to achieve one and the ability to cope with the other."

"It's okay," he said, with a contemplative look on his face. "I think this is better," he continued, as he picked up a pair of dolphins made of porcelain from the uppermost shelf. He didn't need to make much of an effort to reach the topmost shelves; his height was one of the few things he was blessed with.

"No, that's way too common. My choice is much better," she replied in a playful disdain, holding the glass frame in her hand.

Rahul could only manage to nod his head in approval. He couldn't ever go against her.

Keeping the frame back to where she picked it up from, she continued glancing through the hundreds of items kept in that cluttered shop. Rahul consciously tried to look purposefully among the plethora of gift items, wanting to impress her with his sense of judgment. He wanted to seize the God-sent opportunity to show her his smart side – a side he knew didn't exist at all when it came to shopping.

The gift shop was a maze for him and the gift items, doorways; only some of them were legitimate and opened the way to her heart, but most of them were traps which led down to the path of embarrassment. He tried seeking the legitimate ones but was wary of the risk of shame involved in the pursuit.

He had almost given up on the pursuit until his eyes fell upon something which left him spell-bound. On the last shelf of the shop, almost hidden from the view, was kept a figurine of a couple in a loving embrace. It was made of steel with heavy gloss, depicting the nude human forms lost in their moment of intimacy. The lady had her back arched just enough to allow the man to wrap his arms around her back and feel every curve of her body. Her naked breasts touched the man's chest; her hands reached behind the man's neck; the figurine was lifeless and yet Rahul could feel the passion of the moment depicted by it. He felt his own love for Shreya growing stronger by the moment. His emotions got the better of him and he could not help but imagine himself with Shreya in the same stance.

"Hey Shreya, how about his one?" he said, pointing to the figurine. He fought hard to keep his overwhelming emotions under control.

"This? You like this? Come on Rahul, that's not a birthday gift. But your girlfriend would love it," she said, amazed at his choice.

My girlfriend? You will have it in your bedroom very soon, he thought, amazed at his own optimism as he imagined gifting her that showpiece in the near future. He wasn't embarrassed at his idea getting thumbs down from Shreya; he was happy to know that Shreya considered him worthy of a girlfriend.

"How about this Rahul?" she said, diverting his attention to a small, red alarm clock lying at the cash counter. "We will take this," she said to the shop owner, without waiting for his opinion. She paid the bald guy behind the counter two hundred rupees notes, thanked him and made her way to the exit.

Rahul quietly followed behind her, thanking the store owner as he came out of the shop. Shreya, happy at finding a good gift after two hours in the same shop, gambolled to the car with a broad smile on her face. She quickly settled down in the driver's seat, putting her handbag and the gift pack on the rear seat before driving the car out of the cramped lane it was parked in.

Along the way, she was more vivacious than Rahul had ever seen her. She chatted about anything and everything that mattered to her.

"Why doesn't the Indian government do something about these roads? They are such a mess. Rahul, you should do something about it," she said, playfully teasing him.

Not knowing what to say, he just managed to return a smile.

"Are you always this quiet or is it just me?" she asked, with a slight frown while her smile remained intact.

"No, nothing like that," he said, as he shrugged his shoulders, while he touched his left ear in his nervousness to respond to a question he had never been asked before by a girl. He did not know how to explain his diffident manner without sounding a loser. He thought it best to leave it with that ambiguous statement and anxiously tried to divert the attention to some other topic.

"So, you have a boyfriend?" He immediately regretted the statement but knew it was too late to take it back. She had already told him she had a boyfriend, albeit unknowingly. His ears became red with embarrassment.

"Yes," came back the reply, sans any emotions attached. She did not smile, neither did she seem offended. The unusual monosyllabic reply from her made him uneasy. He felt guilty of asking such a question. But what made his heart sink more was the YES, although he already knew she was not single.

He did not expect her to be single; he just wished she was. And his wishes were shattered with the 'yes' from her.

"Do you have a girlfriend?" she asked, catching him off guard. He did not expect her to ask him that. He was always sure that she did not consider him worthy of a girlfriend; the counter question was unexpected and pleasant for him.

"Well….do you think a guy like me can have a girlfriend?" he asked, looking straight ahead on the road, feigning disinterest in her response, waiting for it with bated breath. He wanted to know what she thought about him.

"Yes. You are not that bad. I mean, you are good. So, do you have one?"

The first yes had made him hate the word; the second yes made him fall in love with it all over again.

"No, I don't," he replied, conscious of being as straight-faced as possible.

Maybe she likes me. And maybe, she is lying about having a boyfriend. Girls generally do. But even if she does, I do have a chance. She thinks I am a good guy. Thanks, he thought, as he quietly closed his eyes for a moment, thanking the universe.

"So who all are in your family?" she asked.

"Well, I have a younger brother, father, mother and myself."

"Ok. No sisters?"

"Nopes."

"Maybe that's why you do not have a girlfriend."

"I didn't understand. What is the correlation between me not having a sister and me being single?" he asked, genuinely perplexed at the statement made by her.

"Well, guys with sisters generally understand girls much better and have lesser inhibitions when approaching them. Maybe, you are shy of talking to girls," she said, while she gave her full concentration to the traffic ahead, keeping a firm grip on the steering wheel.

"Or maybe I haven't found a girl yet with whom I would like to get into a relationship," surprised at his own promptness and the defensive statement.

"Okay," she said, with a shrug of her shoulders, raise of the eyebrows and tilt of her head. The reply left him disappointed. He expected her to ask him about the kind of girl he would want to get into a relationship with, which would have given him a chance to profess his liking for her in an obscure manner; but she gave him none.

The conversation they had on their drive back to office was a roller coaster ride for him, making him aware of emotions he had never felt before. And the roller coaster enabled him to get to know her better and more importantly, get to know what she thought about him. He could sense her coming closer to him within the span of half an hour; and his elation knew no bounds.

Back in office, Rahul saw Riya in the same bay as he and Shreya.

"Hey, what are you doing here? Have no work to do or what?" he asked, with a genuine, inquisitive expression on his face.

"I just joined your team," she replied, beaming with delight as she said so. "Isn't it cool?"

"Really? Wow, that's fantastic. That's the second best thing to have happened to me today," Rahul said, as he exchanged high fives with her.

"What is the first?" Riya asked.

"Oh nothing. It's just that I got a couple of hours off from work today, as I had to go shopping for our teammate Prerna," he replied, avoiding eye contact with her. His ears became red as he tried hard to change the topic. He didn't want her to know that he was in love with Shreya.

"But I don't have a clue who Prerna is. Hey, you are an oldie here. Maybe you could introduce us to Prerna," he said, trying to sound as believable as he could while he consciously diverted Riya's attention from his earlier statement.

"Sure. Come dumbo let me introduce you to your team. Call Shreya too, and Hari as well," she said, as she got up from her seat and moved towards the far corner of the bay.

She could sense Rahul's uneasiness at being poked with a 'what' earlier. She desperately wanted to know the reason behind it, but decided to leave it alone for the time being. She knew Rahul too well and didn't want to embarrass him by being pushy. She could sense that his confidence was at an all time high and didn't want to become the reason behind his coming back to his usual diffident self. She knew he would share it with her, whatever it was, when the time's right.

"He is Vikram, our PR guy. He is Ankit, our customer relation executive. She is Prerna, assistant manager, B2B. She is...."

Riya introduced the three of them to every team member, going to their desk one by one, giving a brief info of their respective profiles and what they were responsible for. It hardly mattered to Rahul who all were in his team, as long as Shreya was there, but, nevertheless, he went through the motions, putting on a practiced smile and giving the most confident of handshakes that he could.

The other two got involved in a little chit chat with the complete team. Both of them had their personal and professional motives behind doing it. For Hari, it was personal, for Shreya, it was professional.

Hari had noticed Neha during the introductions, and like 9 girls out of 10, she had aroused him. He cracked a joke or to, gave his own introduction to them, and exchanged little nothings with all, majority being targeted at Neha.

Shreya, being the team leader, engaged with them at a personal level because she thought it would help her manage the team better.

"So you live alone?" she asked one of the guys standing idly in the haphazard circle they had formed unknowingly.

"No, I have my roommates," he replied, rather casually.

"Okay," she replied, as she directed her attention to Prerna. The question-answer session lasted for about 15 minutes, and then it was time for everybody to go home. Rahul had hardly done any work the whole day, but he felt he had accomplished a great deal. The shopping session with Shreya had left him intoxicated. He was in a trance. He packed his bag and set off for home with Hari, jubilant for the day's happening.

"So, how was your shopping with Shreya?" Hari asked, casually, expecting a sombre reply. Rahul was busy laying the table. He had ordered some pizza for dinner for both of them. He hummed a tune as he kept the glasses and the plates on the table, busy with his thoughts and his own happiness.

"Hello, I asked you something. How was your shopping with Shreya?" Hari asked, speaking louder than before, almost on the verge of yelling.

"Hey, don't yell. I am not deaf," Rahul said, irritated. "You know what, it was amazing," he added instantly, not giving Hari a chance to retort with a sarcastic remark.

He hopped onto the bed besides Hari, as he explained to him the day's happenings with the enthusiasm of a kid.

"I think she likes me. I really think she does. And you know what, she even asked me whether I have a girlfriend or not. Isn't that a signal," he said, as a statement, rather than a question.

He was very sure things would only get closer with Shreya from that point onwards.

"What do you think? How should I proceed further? Should I ask for her phone number? No, I think that would be too soon, right?"

He continued blabbering nonstop, hardly pausing for a breath, answering his own questions simultaneously. Hari could only manage a nod of his head at his every statement. He was happy to see him so elated. He patiently sat beside him with a pillow in his lap, his legs crossed, listening to each and every detail being described by Rahul.

"Oh, I guess the dinner is here," Rahul said, as the doorbell rang. "I will get it." He jumped off the bed and a couple of steps later, he was at the door, signing the bill and paying for the order of two large, thin crust pizzas with extra cheese.

It came to 850, which he paid, along with a 100 bucks tip, usually synonymous with someone earning 110 lacs per month, rather than 10,000.

"Cheers to Shreya and Rahul," Hari said, with a wink of his left eye, as they both lifted a slice of their pizzas.

The Heartbreak

I'll ask her about her hobbies today; and her likes and dislikes as well. Rahul thought, as he made plans for the day, while he combed his hair and got ready for office. *What if she asks me the same? Hmmm, if she says she likes partying, I would say the same too. And if she says she loves to read books, I would say I love reading romance.*

Yes! Satisfied with his planning, he punched his fist in the air, locked the main door and stood at the gate, waiting for Hari.

But what if she asks me the question first? he thought, perplexed at the new situation that his expectations presented before him.

Listening to music, watching movies, and hanging out with friends. That should be fine I guess, he thought, fully aware that they were hardly his hobbies. He wanted to play it safe. He didn't want to ruin the beginning he had got with her. He was too afraid to lose her and didn't want to say anything that could make her feel that he was just an ordinary guy.

He consciously tried to manipulate his thoughts, coming up with situations and rehearsing answers for each of them. He was still thinking of plausible situations, unaware of his changing facial expressions with his every thought, when Hari broke his train with a loud honk.

"Let's go Mr. lover. Else, we might be late for office," Hari shouted in order to get his voice heard over the blaring music which was coming out from a car parked nearby.

They reached office half an hour before the scheduled reporting time. There was hardly anybody around except the familiar faces they had encountered on day one. Rahul was glad to see that Shreya had not arrived, and neither had Riya, as it gave him more time to rehearse his expected conversation with the girl he was madly in love with.

Hey up there. Please guide me through the rest of it. You know I love her and my love is really true. I trust you, and I know you are always there with me. He prayed, with his eyes closed, smiling visibly as he said the last line.

With his faith reaffirmed, he switched on his system, entered his username and password, and waited for the system to boot.

Hari quickly logged on to his favourite porn site to get his daily dose of adult adventure. But even before he could get a decent erection, he heard footsteps approaching the bay, which forced him to close the website and open his mailbox instead.

It was Riya, dressed in a simple white tee and a pair of blue jeans. "Hi dumbo, what's up?" she said, as she lovingly slapped Rahul on the back of his head.

"Me fantastic as usual. You tell me, How are you? And how come you so early? There are still minutes to go to reporting time."

"Just like that. I thought I should go early for a change," Riya replied, as she shook hands with Hari.

"How are you Hari?"

"Me good. You tell me," Hari replied, successfully managing to hide his disappointment at not getting enough porn for the day because of her intrusion.

"Me good too," she replied casually, as she settled into her chair, which was to the left of Rahul.

"Hey, there's still time yaar. Come, let's go grab a coffee," Riya said to Rahul, after she switched on her PC and was waiting for it to boot.

"Okay, let's go. Hey Hari, come, let's go for a coffee," Rahul said, and grabbed Hari by the arm without waiting for his response.

The three of them walked towards the elevator, as the cafeteria was on the first floor of the building.

"So dumbo, liking your new life?" Riya asked Rahul, with an expression that expected a yes for an answer.

"Absolutely. I love it," Rahul replied, exchanging a quick glance with Hari and a smirk.

"And what about you Mr.? How are you adjusting to your new life?" she asked Hari, as they stepped into the elevator.

"Oh, it's good," Hari replied, not knowing what to answer for that question, as he himself wasn't sure whether he was happy with his new life or not.

Ten seconds later. The elevator stopped on the first floor. Rahul waited for Riya to exit the elevator first and forced Hari to do the same.

"Get some manners dude," Rahul whispered in Hari's ears, grabbing his arm tightly, while Riya exited the elevator.

The cafeteria was bang in front of the elevator and it was teeming with people.

“Who are all these people? There is no sign of people back down,” Rahul said aloud, in a genuinely curious tone of voice.

“Oh, these are the call centre people. Their shift gets over at 09:30 and they usually have breakfast at the cafeteria before they leave,” Riya replied promptly, matter-of-factly, used to seeing such crowd everyday. Hari and Riya took a table at the centre of the cafeteria, while Rahul went to the counter to order coffee for the three of them.

“So you know Rahul from college, right?” Riya asked Hari.

“Yes,” was the monosyllabic reply she got from him.

“So is this your first job too?”

“Oh no. I worked for HCL earlier,” Hari replied.

“Okay. Don’t mind, but why did you quit? I mean, I am not interviewing you or something. I am asking just like that. You can skip that if you want to,” Riya said, conscious of the fact that she did not intrude the privacy of a relatively unknown guy.

“Oh no, I don’t have a problem with that,” he replied, biting his lower lip simultaneously as he searched for an answer.

He did not want to reveal the reason behind leaving his earlier job to anyone in Hewlett-Packard so soon. He was wary of the reactions he would get when people would get to know that he had been accused of passing sexual remarks on a colleague in his earlier company, which was the reason behind him leaving the job. It was another matter that he had been falsely accused, but he found it hard to convince people about that after they heard the ‘s’ word.

"What's going on?" Rahul said, as he came to the table, balancing three cups of coffee in two hands.

Hari heaved a sigh of relief and thanked God for Rahul's intervention.

"Oh, nothing much. Just passing time," Riya replied.

"Okay."

"So dumbo, did you find any girlfriend for yourself or not?" Riya asked Rahul, with a wide grin and a glint in her eyes. She knew she would get a non for an answer and that would give her the opportunity to pull his leg, something which she loved doing.

"Nyah," Rahul replied, looking at his cup of coffee rather than at Riya.

"You are an asshole. You don't have the guts to go talk to a girl. In our case too, I was the one who talked to you first. I don't know how you are going to talk to your wife even," Riya said with a grin, indulging in some good old banter with her school buddy.

"Whatever," Rahul replied, as he tried to brush the subject under the carpet. Hari enjoyed a short laugh himself, seeing Riya get the upper hand on his buddy.

Riya enjoyed Rahul's irritability at the subject. She always enjoyed bullying him, because she knew Rahul would never take it as an offence.

Rahul lifted his gaze forcefully from the coffee cup to Riya's eyes to show her he was not afraid of taking her comments head-on. But his gaze went beyond Riya, towards the door of the cafeteria.

Shreya, wearing a red chequered shirt and slim fit jeans with a belt around her waist, was approaching their table.

She waved a 'hi' to him, and he waved her back, with a sheepish grin.

"Hi Hari. Hi Riya. Good morning everyone," she said, as she bent a little, resting her one hand on the table while she shook the other with the three of them. Rahul quickly grabbed a vacant chair from the adjoining table and kept it besides Shreya.

"Oh, thank you so much," Shreya said, and settled down in the chair.

"Want to have coffee?" Rahul asked eagerly, wanting to showcase his leadership skills.

"No, not really. It's almost time. I actually found nobody in the office except your bag, so I came down to the cafeteria, as I guessed you would be here."

"Okay," Rahul replied, with a grin that wouldn't come to an end. He felt proud and important at knowing that she had come looking for him.

"So, shall we leave?" Riya said, and stood up from the chair immediately. Rahul was the next one to get up and he stood right beside Shreya, waiting for Hari to get up too.

The office was starting to fill up, with greetings being shouted to one another and tasks being assigned. The four of them took their respective seats and began sifting through their mail boxes, looking for any important mails that might have dropped in. There were none for any of them. Hari, Rahul and Shreya got on with their mundane tasks they had been assigned on the first day of their joining, while Riya, being the old bloke, decided to exchange greetings with almost everybody on the floor.

Wow. She came to the canteen looking for me. Thanks universe. It's happening. I would ask her about her hobbies at lunchtime. Rahul thought, getting goose bumps at the thought that he had made some sort of an image in front of her. He tried hard to concentrate on the job at hand, but couldn't. He was preoccupied visualising the conversation with her.

Great. So you like sketching. How about sketching my face someday?

Well, sure, I would love to.

You know what, you are different. Guys are not usually into painting and sketching stuff. They are more into sports. But you are an exception. I like that.

He pictured many such conversations with Shreya, while trying to focus on his computer screen, but in vain.

I would ask her the hobby question at lunch. It will give me more time to interact with her. He thought, as he gave a quick glance to his right, where Shreya was busy typing out a document.

○○○

"Hey dumbo, let's go for lunch," Riya said, as she picked up her lunchbox. It was almost 2:00 p.m. Hari got up from his seat too, and stood beside Riya, waiting for Rahul to get up.

"Oh come on, let's go. I am feeling hungry," Hari said, exasperated.

"Let Shreya come," Rahul said, like an innocent kid waiting for his mother to get back from the market.

Shreya was not at her desk. She had gone to Varsha, the project manager, to get some important stuff sorted out.

"Oh come now, we will call her. Let's find a table first," Hari said, forcefully shutting down Rahul's computer while literally dragging him to the cafeteria. The cafeteria was buzzing with people, and all the tables were occupied except one.

"There's one table. And it has exactly four chairs. Lucky us," Riya said.

"I'll grab the table. You two go get your meal." Riya went across to the table and kept her lunch box on one chair, her handbag on the second, her mobile on the third, and sat on the last one left.

Being bachelors and living alone, Hari and Rahul didn't get their lunches from home, although both of them knew a little bit of cooking. Both of them took their plates and stood in line at the food counter, waiting for their turn to fill up their plates.

"Hari, you said you would call Shreya. Call her. It's bad manners to have lunch without your team leader," Rahul said, in a desperate tone of voice.

"Oh really?" Hari replied, raising his eyebrows, giving a wry smile, making mockery of Rahul's desperation. "But I don't have her number. Sorry."

"You asshole," Rahul said, punching him hard on his left shoulder.

"Chill dude. There, look. She's already there with Riya."

Rahul saw Riya and Shreya chatting animatedly at the table. He heaved a sigh of relief. His conversation plan did not need to be changed. Rahul and Hari filled the plates with almost identical stuff – rice, *dal*, two chapattis and curd – and joined the two girls at the table.

"How mean you guys are. You did not even wait for me," Shreya said, giggling simultaneously along with Riya.

"I told them to wait for you. I am the good one here," Rahul said, eager to prove his innocence.

"Hmm," was all that Shreya replied, without making a direct eye contact with him.

Rahul saw her eating engrossingly. She had brought some boiled rice along with curd, and he could sense her contentment and her happiness at having that simple meal. But the cold response from her made his negative emotions come to the surface.

Maybe I spoke it too fast. Or maybe she just takes me as a colleague and nothing else, he thought. His heart took a nosedive with that thought, which made him chew very slowly, albeit unconsciously.

Hell, she said she came looking for me in the morning. She likes me. His spirits pepped up again when he thought about the conversation he had in the morning. And with his confidence regained, he decided to go ahead with his luncheon conversation plan.

"So Shreya, what are your hobbies like?" he asked, rather abruptly, interrupting the conversation of her and Riya. The question prompted a look of perplexity on the faces of all three of them, which made Rahul conscious of his bad timing.

"Well, um, listening to music, dancing, going to parties and um, watching movies," she replied, and got back to her conversation with Riya.

Okay, mine are going to parties and watching movies now, Rahul thought, as he waited for Shreya to ask her the same question.

The question never came.

Rahul could sense her indifference and decided not to pursue the conversation further. He finished his lunch quietly and was the first one to get off the table, while the other three were still having theirs.

"What happened?" the three of them asked in unison.

"Oh, nothing, have some important work. You guys carry on," Rahul said, feigning his dejection at being ignored by Shreya by putting on a faint smile and showing fake urgency.

He threw his plate in the dustbin and quickly made his way back downstairs, fighting hard to keep back the tears that were welling inside him.

Why can't you tell me whether she likes me or not? When will you stop playing games with me? The inner voice shouted inside him, as it fought with the universe for the right answer.

When you want something wholeheartedly, the whole univer....he shut the voice inside him that asked him to keep faith in love.

They had ordered some south Indian food for dinner from a roadside stall nearby. Newspapers were spread all over the bed. Hari served some *sambhar* and *idli* in each of the plates, while Rahul played with the tuner of the radio, searching for an FM channel that played some songs.

"So dude, how is it going with Shreya huh?" Hari said, as he settled down in one corner of the bed and tucked into his dinner.

There was no response. Rahul slowly broke a piece of *idli*, dipped it in *sambhar* and had his first bite of dinner.

ooo

"ooooooo … lovey dovey huh. Can't get her out of your head, Mr. Lover boy," Hari continued, without paying any heed to his lack of response.

There was silence.

"Hey, why don't you ask her out on a date?" Hari asked, giving a snigger and a pat on Rahul's lap.

"She even said she was looking for you in the morning," Hari continued, "huh, bastard you," he said, nudging Rahul, in a teasing, playful manner.

Tears rolled down from Rahul's eyes.

"She doesn't like me," Rahul sobbed. "It's all bullshit. She just takes me to be a good colleague", Rahul said, as he continued sobbing, his tone that of dejection and irritation.

He put down his fork and rested his head in between his legs, crying uncontrollably. Never been subjected to such a situation before, Hari didn't know how to respond. He felt sorry for inadvertently hurting his feelings and felt more so, as he did not know of a way to console him.

He tried putting his hand on his shoulders, in order to show his support, but was forcefully shrugged off.

"Hey, come on, she likes you. Trust me. I know how girls are. Her indifference is her way of showing that she likes you. That's how girls usually are," Hari said, with as much conviction as he could bring himself to.

He knew what he was saying was bullshit, but all he cared for at that moment was to help his friend calm down.

But his good natured lying came to nothing. Rahul continued crying, without paying any heed to his words. Hari decided to call Riya, unable to handle the situation himself. "Hello," he said hurriedly, as Riya answered the call.

"Yes," she replied. "Riya, Hari here. We have got a problem at hand."

"What happened?"

He explained to her everything about Rahul's love for Shreya, his spending time with her, and indifference shown on her part.

"Give the phone to him please," Riya said.

"Hello," Rahul said, after Hari handed him the phone. He was still sobbing.

"Hey dumbo, listen to me. You are a damn good guy. You would win her for sure. I would help you do that, promise. But only on one condition – you have to stop crying," she said, trying hard to calm him down.

Her words worked. Rahul listened to her intently, without speaking anything in response. He didn't want to say anything to anybody. He was too heartbroken to speak.

"Thanks," he said abruptly, in a lowly voice, interrupting her, "Good night Riya. Go to sleep. It's already late," he said.

"Okay. You too should go to sleep. Bye dumbo, and take care", she said, and hung up the phone, praying to God to give him strength to cope with it.

The Second Chance

The next day Rahul didn't feel like going to office, but Hari goaded him to come along.

"Come on buddy, it's okay. She likes you. Trust me," Hari said, not sure himself whether he should be saying so when he had no clue about how to read girls.

"Remember, universe always gives you the things you want badly. You always tell me that. Have faith in the universe", he added, trying to make Rahul get up from bed and get ready for office.

"You don't need to say all that. I know she does not like me. I will come to office, don't worry. You go, I'll come a little later," said Rahul, with a passive face, without even batting an eyelid. He looked straight up at the ceiling, as if searching for an answer to the only question he had in mind – *Will she ever be mine?*

Feeling bad for leaving him alone, Hari drags himself out of his room and gets in his car to go to office. *How can people love somebody so much? He is crazy. Physical need is the basis of life. Why can't we all be happy with getting physical pleasure alone? Why do most of us have to fall in the emotional trap? That's secondary. Shreya's physical beauty is what attracted him in the first place, emotions came after that.* Hari thought, while driving his car slower than the usual.

It was almost half an hour beyond the reporting time when Hari reached office. The floor was buzzing with activity, and Shreya was there too, typing frantically, while looking at her computer screen.

Hari felt a certain kind of animosity towards her, but didn't know the reason behind it. He said a formal 'hi' while he walked past her. The usual bonhomie was missing in the 'hi'. He shook hands with Riya, who was there too and settled down in his seat.

"How is Rahul?" asked Riya in a whispering tone and a concerned expression on her face.

"Bad," said Hari, with a shake of his head. "But he is coming to office."

"Okay. That's good."

"Hey Hari, Rahul is not coming today?" asked Shreya, taking a break from her typing.

"No," said Hari.

"Why? What happened? Is he okay?" she asked, with a genuine concern on her face.

Hari wanted to tell her all about last night and how she was the reason behind his sadness. He wanted to let her know how much Rahul loved her and how indifferent she had been to him.

"He is okay. He has some personal stuff to take care of. He will come a little later," he said, fighting the urge to let out his frustration at her.

"Okay," she said with a smile and returned to her computer screen.

"Why are you angry at her? It's not her fault", said Riya. She noticed his stern expression and monosyllabic answers spoken without any intonation.

"I am not angry. Who said I am angry? I am Mr. cool, always remember that," Hari said, using his pretentious devil-may-care attitude as a veil against his irritation with the concept of love.

OOO

It was 2:00 p.m., Shreya, Riya and Hari logged off from their systems and got ready to go to the cafeteria for lunch.

Hari was the first to log off, and he stood with his hands on his hips, waiting for the girls to do the same. He looked around the floor to overcome his impatience, and as his eyes went to the glass door, he could see a lanky figure, dressed in white shirt and blue jeans, droopily making his way to the bay he was standing in. It was Rahul. He waved a 'hi' to Hari as he slowly made his way to his bay.

"Hey, hi Rahul, what's up?" said Shreya, in a cheerful tone, as if pleasantly surprised at seeing him.

"I'm good," he said, quickly making his way past her.

"We were just about to leave for lunch. Come, join us," said Shreya.

"No. I have already had my lunch. Carry on," he said. He didn't look at her as he said so.

"You sure you don't want to join us?"asked Riya.

"Yes," said Rahul, with rapid blinking of his eyes.

"Okay, come then, let's go," said Riya, and the three of them made their way to the cafeteria.

She didn't even ask me a second time. She doesn't like me, thought Rahul, and sank into his seat.

OOO

Days were passing by and Rahul was getting accustomed to his daily schedule. His work took precedence over everything else and he was slowly coming to terms with the fact that Shreya and he could just be colleagues and nothing else, although he still harboured faith in the universe and longed for the day when his love would win. His logical senses told him something else and he was beginning to reconcile with them, without leaving his emotional senses alone.

It had almost been a month since he had joined office, and throughout the one month, he hadn't seen a single day when Shreya hadn't come to office on time.

Sitting in the bay, with people milling around and his computer's clock showing eleven, he felt uneasy about the absence of Shreya to his right.

"Riya, has Shreya informed you that she won't be coming or something?" he asked, twitching his eyebrows and cracking his knuckles.

"Nopes," Riya said, smiling at his concern, and got back to reading a document.

She should have informed somebody at least. What could have happened? he thought, staring blankly at the screen. His mind did not reveal any plausible causes; there was just emptiness inside, except the concern.

He pretended to read some important stuff on his system in order to take his mind away from her, and failed miserably. He wanted to call her, but didn't have her number. He knew he could get it from Riya, but didn't want to. *Hari would think I am a loser.*

But his desperation urged him to call her, and his desperation got the better of him.

"Riya, do you have her number?" he asked.

"Yes. Just wait. Let me search in my cellphone."

"Here it is. Its 9876546321," she said, giving him Shreya's number.

"Thanks," he said, and typed the digits on his cellphone.

And just as he was about to dial the number, he saw her coming. It was the same graceful walk he had seen on the first day of office, but he could sense something amiss.

Keeping her bag down on the table, she switched on her computer and settled down in her chair.

"Hi Rahul," she said, without a smile.

"Hi Riya, hi Hari," she waved a 'hi' to each of them, without making any attempt at smiling.

What's the matter with her? Something is wrong, Rahul thought, noticing her change in behaviour.

"How come so late today?" he asked.

"Oh, nothing. A huge traffic jam. A truck had broken down, so got late for work," she said, with a straight face, and a muted tone.

"Ok." *She is lying. What could be the matter? Should I ask her?* He thought, asking questions to his own self. What *if she thinks I am intruding her privacy? Let it be.* He answered his own questions.

He continued with his work but couldn't concentrate. He kept glancing at her after every few minutes, as if trying to decipher the reason behind her unhappiness. He found none.

She was busy typing on her computer, writing an important document that the project manager has asked for.

OOO

Just half an hour was left for the day to get over and everybody was busy wrapping up things and getting up to leave. Everybody, except Shreya. She was engrossed in her cellphone, tapping the keys one after the other, seemingly looking for something.

Rahul glanced at her, and he could feel the sadness on her face. Slowly, the sadness became visible to all. Tears started rolling down her cheeks; she started sobbing, still looking at her mobile's screen.

"Hey, what happened?" Riya asked, rushing by her side. She put her arm on her shoulder, trying to calm her down, while she kept repeating the same question. Shreya continued sobbing, without giving anybody the reason behind it.

"What happened Shreya? Is everything okay at home?" Rahul asked, fighting back the tears that were welling in his eyes.

"Yes. I just want to go home," she said, picking up her bag, and got up to leave.

"Okay. Hari will drop you," Rahul said, as he gave Hari a quick glance, as if instructing him to obey his command.

"I have to go somewhere urgent. Rahul, why don't you drop her home?" Hari said. He didn't have anything urgent. All he wanted was to give Rahul a chance to get close to her. He didn't believe in her, but desperately wanted Rahul's love to win over everything else.

"Okay. Let's go. You stop crying, ok. Everything will be alright," Rahul said, as he took Shreya's car keys from her bag and escorted her to the car, which was parked in front of the main gate. Shreya settled in the passenger's seat while Rahul got in the driver's seat of the car.

She was still sobbing, tears rolling down her cheeks sporadically.

"Here, have some water," he offered her the water bottle he had picked up from Riya on his way outside.

"Thanks," she said, and took a small sip.

"Are you alright now?" He asked, seeing that she relatively calmed down.

"Yes."

"Good," he said, and started the car to take her home.

"Please tell me the way."

"Okay."

Those were the only sentences exchanged between them till it was almost half an hour's driving that Rahul had done. He could no longer keep himself from asking the reason behind her sadness.

"Shreya, if you have ever considered me a friend of yours, please tell me what's the matter," he said, knowing that 'friend' was too risky a word to use. They hadn't ever used the word in whatever conversations they had had, and he wasn't sure if Shreya considered him anything more than a colleague. Still, he took a chance.

"I broke up with my boyfriend," was the stern response he got from her.

He could see the dejection on her face as she said so. He felt sorry for her. Even though his logical part told him it was a good development for him, he could not bring himself to rejoice at that news. He wanted to see her happy, and the sorrow eyes and the solemn expression he found on her face at that moment made him disgusted of himself for even thinking of rejoicing.

He forgot how indifferently she had treated him a while back; he forgot that he wanted her badly in his life; he forgot that it might be an opportunity thrown by the universe his way; all he wanted was to see her happy and he was ready to do anything for that. He wanted to hug her tightly and ask her to have faith in the universe. He wanted to hold her hand and tell her how the person who betrayed her did not deserve her. But he couldn't do so.

"I'm sorry. But you know what; you are a damn good person. And you will definitely find a guy who wants to spend the rest of his life with you. Trust me," he said, smiling, trying to cheer her up.

"Really? Do you think so?"

"Yup."

"Thanks. This way," she said, guiding him to her place.

"Stop, stop, stop."

"Okay. So this is where you stay," Rahul said, as he came to a stop in front of an apartment complex.

"Yes."

"Should I park the car inside or....?"

"No. You have done so much already. I'll take care of that."

"Sure?"

"Yup."

"Okay."

She got out of the car and stood by the driver's side of the car. Rahul got out too, handed her the keys and turned around to leave for home.

"Uh ... Rahul!" Shreya said.

"Yes," he replied, turning around to know what the matter was. He slowly walked towards her. "Any problem?"

"No. Just wanted to say thank you," she said, and hugged him tightly.

He didn't know how to react. He was frozen at the moment. He couldn't move his arms to wrap around her body. He stood there, motionless, not knowing what had hit him.

"Bye," he said, as he fidgeted with the button of his shirt's sleeves.

He turned around and walked as fast as he could, to get away from her quickly. He began crying uncontrollably. He himself wasn't sure about the reason behind his tears. He didn't know whether he was sad or happy. He was overwhelmed with her gesture. Not sure how he would reach his room at that hour of the night, without any conveyance with him, he kept on walking at a frantic pace, occasionally wiping off tears with his bare hands.

ooo

A few days passed by, but Shreya found it hard to overcome her break up. She tried to immerse herself in work, but in vain. She tried to stay surrounded with her colleagues, but that didn't help her either. Her being alone at her place made matters worse. It was not as if she was living alone for the first time in her life; but the emotional loneliness that she felt haunted her.

Sitting in front of her desktop, she just blankly stared at her screen, until her eyes ached.

As Rahul glances at her, he feels a strong empathy towards her. He could understand better than anybody else what she was going through. He went through the same feelings not so long ago. And despite being heartbroken himself; he wanted to lend out an arm around Shreya and make her understand how special she was. He wanted to convey a million things to her to make her happy; but didn't know how. And just then, the universe intervened.

Suddenly looking away from the computer screen and towards Rahul, she said, "Would you mind going out for a movie with me tomorrow?"

Rahul could feel the innocence on her face and her helplessness at that moment. He forgot the embarrassment he had faced after spending the happiest day of his life, shopping with her. He forgot the ignorance he had to face at her hands. He forgot how she had unknowingly played with his feelings.

His ego shouted inside him – *Don't do the mistake again. She would ruin you. Remember, how she treated you the last time around? She doesn't love you. She is selfish. All she cares for is her own feelings. Do not say a yes this time.*

But he couldn't hear a word his ego was saying to him. All he could see was that his love was helpless at that moment and she wanted his help. Without a semblance of doubt in his mind, "Yeah sure. Why not! How about *Sixth Sense*? I heard its good", he said, at his happiest best, glad that he had the chance to be the reason for her solace in times of discomfort. Her condition reminded him of his own self a month back, and helping her out made him feel as if he was alleviating his own troubles.

"Great. Thank you so much," she said, a genuine smile breaking across her face for the first time in the past few days.

The next day, Rahul borrowed Hari's car and picked her up from her place at eleven in the morning. The show was to start at one, and they had ample time to reach the theatre, which was half an hour's drive from her place, and buy the tickets. Shreya was casually dressed in a pink tee and blue jeans, while Rahul was wearing the best clothes he had in his wardrobe, which were not very great in terms of style. But dressing up in the best that he had always made him confident and self-assured, and he was feeling the same that day.

They reached the theatre at 11:45. To their utter surprise, there was a long queue outside the ticket window. They had heard that the movie was a big hit, but had not anticipated such a crowd for the movie.

"Gosh. Look at that man. What the f...." he grimaced, with sheer amazement.

"Don't freak. It's a weekend. Come, we will get the ticket. Don't worry. It's not that long," she said.

Rahul parked the car in the crammed parking space and stood in the queue, while Shreya stood by his side to give him company.

They both stood in silence, waiting for their turn to buy the ticket. Feeling uncomfortable standing quiet for so long, Shreya turned around and looked at the crowd, which was increasing every minute. And while looking at the crowd, she noticed a bunch of her old friends who were standing in the queue.

She quickly left Rahul and gambolled towards them. They were a group of four guys, same age as hers. She hugged all four of them tightly, one after the other, and chatted with them animatedly. Rahul, who had turned around to see where she was going, felt a pulse of anger and disappointment growing inside him, seeing her behaviour with the guys standing not far back from him.

She doesn't care about me. She would leave me as soon as she finds somebody else. Am I just a puppet for her? Am I just somebody who is there to fill the place when there is nobody for her? Am I just a stopgap solution for her?

He started questioning himself on his own actions. His ego resurfaced, and tried to make him aware of the futility of his actions. He tried hard to ignore it, but her behaviour did not allow him to do so.

A strange sense of disappointment and rage started building inside him, and he feared that he could explode any minute, with the combined pressure of anger and regret at his own actions. And just then, Shreya returned, taking her position by his side.

He quickly turned around, facing the ticket window again, casually and calmly waiting for his turn, as if he had not noticed her going away. After waiting for fifteen minutes in the queue, they got the ticket for the movie; and both of them proceeded to the waiting lounge, keeping a small distance between themselves, as they walked towards it.

"Thanks again! You're really good," she said, as they sat in the lounge, waiting for the gates to open.

He could see the truth in her eyes when she thanked him and it made him feel proud. He felt as if he had done the noblest deed in the world. Her happiness meant the world to him, and he was glad that his actions helped her get over her grief.

The gates opened at exactly 1 o'clock, and they both proceeded towards their designated seats, Rahul protecting her from the jostling and pushing going around at the entry gate. He keeps her in front and puts both his hands on her shoulders, as if to signify that he was always behind her whenever she needed him. It made him feel important. They were allotted the corner seats in the third last row of the hall.

A six year old girl, dressed in blue overalls slowly approaches the camera. Her eyes begin to turn red as she starts to show signs of insane violence. With her gaze fixed on the camera, she gives a tap on the shoulder of the man standing with his back to her. There's a scream, and the screen turns red.

Shreya clutches on to Rahul's arm after seeing the opening scene of the movie. She keeps looking at the screen, her brows furrowed, sitting in a cringing position, her arms wrapped tightly around Rahul's. It was a horror movie and Shreya watched the entire show holding on to him.

Thank you up there. Rahul thanked God for giving him those moments with her. He was glad that he came to the movie with her. And he wished that the movie would never come to an end. He wanted those moments to last for an eternity. But to his disappointment, the movie came to an abrupt end two hours later. It was time for them to go home, and the thought of leaving her made him anxious. He wasn't sure whether he would get the chance to spend such moments with her ever again; nevertheless, he had to do the painful thing of saying goodbye to her.

He dropped her at her place, and it made him feel as if he had lost a vital part of his own self. He felt as if he had lost something which was vital for his existence, and that he should turn back and bring back the thing. But he couldn't.

The Heartbreak Again

Rahul, Riya, Shreya and Hari start bonding well together. Their conversations move away from the lunch table alone. They spend most of their time together, shopping, roaming, eating and indulging in good fun. They become a close knit unit, enjoying each other's company. Rahul gets to spend a lot of time with Shreya, in the presence of the other two, and pounces at every opportunity he gets to catch her attention. However, to his dismay, Shreya still maintains a distance from him, preferring indulging in group activities that involved the four of them. Shreya finally gets over her break up and enjoys every minute of her time spent with the three of them. They even celebrate Riya's birthday together, deciding to go pub hopping.

They have a blast of a time, and all four of them agree to repeat it very soon. They rarely call each other by their names. They have their own code names given by each other. Shreya is called "Miss Makeup", for her fondness to apply makeup all the time; Riya is called "Crazy Ball", for her effervescent nature; Hari is called "Hunter", for his irritating habit of always for girls to go to bed with him; and Rahul is called "Lalloo Ram", for his simple nature.

ооо

26th March, Sunday.

It's Shreya's birthday. Rahul called her up in the morning, and gave her the greetings of the day.

"Happy birthday. What are you doing?" were the first words he spoke when she answered the call.

"Hey Rahul. Thanks. Nothing much, just got up," she replied.

"Okay, cool. So what are the plans for the day?" he asked, expecting an invitation from her for her birthday party. All he got was disappointment.

"Nothing as of now," was the blunt response he got.

Rahul understood her unwillingness to invite him to the party and hangs up, saying a casual goodbye to her.

She could have said she would let me know. But she didn't. Maybe, she actually does not have any plans. Let's call her in the evening. I am sure she would invite me if she had a party. After all, I was there with her when she was down. I know she would. He thought, contradicting his own disappointment.

He eagerly awaits the clock to tick and the earth to move. Being a Sunday, he had plenty of time to kill, and didn't have the means. He decided to go to Hari's place in order to pass his time, until the time came to call her up. He put on his pyjamas, a regular t-shirt and set foot to Hari's place.

"Hey, what's up? How come you here?" Hari said, after he opened the door and found Rahul standing at the door, to his surprise.

"Had nothing to do. So decided I should come here," Rahul replied, barging straight in, without waiting for an invitation.

He threw himself on his bed, and began fiddling with his laptop. He opened various windows that were minimised, and much to his expectations, found hardcore porn running in all of them.

"Oh shit. When would you stop all this? Come on, you are twenty-three now. Have some shame, you filthy animal," Rahul said, punching Hari hard on his left shoulder. Hari grimaced in pain and quietly shut down his laptop.

"Leave that. What's the plan?" Hari asked, deliberately changing the topic.

"Nothing. We will have lunch and then listen to some music, and that's it," Rahul replied.

"Okay. Cool."

They both ordered a simple meal from a nearby restaurant and had food to their heart's content, indulging in playful bantering all along. They both took digs at each other and both of them enjoyed it.

As planned, Hari switched on some good music on his laptop, and both of them enjoyed listening to it, falling back on the pillows and enjoying the energy of the rock songs that Hari had in his collection. None of them spoke a word, and yet, they were as comfortable with their own silence and the sound of the music, as a new born in his mother's lap.

Rahul lost track of time listening to some soft and hard rock, and didn't realise that it was evening, until he casually glanced at the clock hanging on the wall, which showed 5:30. He fumbled through his pocket for his mobile phone.

Tring, Tring....Tring, Tring ... he impatiently waited for her to pick up the phone.

"Hello," came the voice from the other end.

"Hi," he said.

"Hi," she replied, casually. "You have already wished me, remember?" she added.

"Yeah, I do remember. Was getting bored, so just wanted to know which place we should go to celebrate your birthday," he said, speaking only half the truth.

"Oh. I am actually with my cousins right now. They have come over at my place today," she said, wanting to add more to it but Rahul interrupted her.

"Oh, ok. No problems," he said, hiding his dejection behind his casualness. He hangs up.

Tears well up in his eyes and questions again start pondering his mind.

Am I not worthy enough to meet her cousins? Doesn't she think I am good enough to meet her relatives? Am I that bad? He starts thinking, getting lost in the maze of his own thoughts, looking for answers.

"What happened?" Everything alright?" Hari asks, concerned, looking at his uneasiness.

He starts snivelling, speaking at the same time.

"Am I not good enough for her?" he asks.

"You are damn good. What happened?"

"She doesn't consider me worthy enough to be invited at her birthday party."

"Come on. She must not be having one. You are one of her closest friends, remember? She asked for your company when she was feeling low. Why wouldn't she invite you to her party? Come, let's go for a drink. It would make you feel better. Let's go," Hari said, and dragged him out of the bed.

Rahul picked up the gift he had bought for her and followed Hari. They both went to the hippest pub in town to catch a drink.

The music was playing loud and the strobe lights were flashing all over the place. It took them a couple of minutes to acclimatise themselves to the dim interiors, after which they approached the bar and sat down. They both ordered a beer for themselves, and their chairs towards the dance floor, which was jam-packed, even though it was just 7:00 p.m.

They raised their glasses, said casual cheers, and had a huge sip from their respective glasses.

"You were right. Maybe she isn't having a party at all. Thanks for taking me out," Rahul said. He was starting to feel better and was beginning to believe that Shreya wasn't celebrating her birthday. Just then, his belief came crashing down.

He saw Shreya in the crowd, dancing with a group of friends. Dressed in an off shoulder black top and a mid length skirt, with high heeled stilettos, she looked stunning. Looking across the dance floor, their eyes met.

But she continued dancing with her friends, enjoying the music.

Rahul got off the chair, grabbed the gift he had mistakenly brought inside the pub and walked towards her. It took him more than just self-control to not let tears roll down his cheeks. He made his way through the crowded dance floor, pushing and shoving people, until he reached her.

He wanted to grab her arm and ask her the reason for the treatment she meted out to him. He wanted to cry out loud in front of her and let her know how much she had hurt him. But he did nothing. Instead, he wished her a curt birthday again, and handed her the gift. His face didn't show any emotions at all – neither of regret, nor of sorrow; neither of sadness, nor of disappointment. He didn't want her to know what he was going through.

He turned back and exited the pub, without waiting for Hari.

"Hey, beer is still left," Hari shouted, calling him back in. But he knew he wouldn't. He gulped down both the glasses of beer in front of him and hurried after Rahul.

They didn't speak a word on their way back. Hari was feeling guilty for infusing false optimism in his best friend. He felt sorry for giving him false hopes, and his guilt didn't allow him to console his buddy. He thought it best to leave him to his own thoughts, and pray for time to take its own course. He dropped him at his place and went his way.

After a hard night of partying, Shreya came back to her place at 12 at night, slightly drunk. She couldn't recall that she had seen Rahul at the pub; but she does remember that the gift wrapped in green in her hand was given by him. Too tired to change clothes, she falls back on the bed, and tears the green wrapping apart. She carefully opens the box embossed with golden letters in bold, 'L'oreal'. It was a make up kit, with a chit inside that read – "Happy birthday, Miss Makeup."

A smile breaks across her face and she keeps the box by her bedside table. She takes off her stilettos, pulls the bed sheet from under her and goes to sleep, in the same clothes that she had partied in.

Love is Forgiving

Rahul and Hari arrived at their usual time at office. There's almost an eerie silence in the office, as if employees had deserted the place long ago. They expected to see the usual faces they encountered everyday when they arrived first – the same guy still hoping to ace tetris; the same face checking out hot videos of Pamela Anderson on the internet; and a few other faces going about their routine tasks in their usual manner.

But that morning, there was an unfamiliar face for that hour of the day. It was Shreya. She had come early and was already scanning through her e-mails, sorting out the stuff and prioritising it. She smiled at both of them as they stepped in. Hari smiled back, while Rahul's face was passive. He hadn't gotten over the happenings of last night and that made him go into his shell all over again.

"Hey Rahul, thanks for the gift. That was so sweet of you," she said, as Rahul pulled his chair and settled in.

No response came from him, not even facially.

"Hey, I am sorry," she said, with the same innocence on her face which she displayed, when she asked him out for a movie.

"Sorry for what?" Rahul retorted sarcastically, his anger and frustration palpable through his words.

"I know you felt bad that I didn't invite you to the party. But it's just that I had already committed to some other friends of mine, and they had made me promise that I won't invite anyone else."

"You could have told me that, couldn't you?" he questioned, being open about his feelings for her for the first time since he met her.

"I thought you might feel bad about the whole stuff. I didn't know that you would come to the same pub. I was hiding it only because I didn't want you to feel as if you are inferior to my other friends."

No response came.

"Forgive me, please," she pleaded, clasping her hands together.

There was still no response.

"Okay. What do you want? A treat? Okay, we'll go to Pizza Hut today. Fine?"

He was oblivious to what she was saying. His mind kept running back to the night before, when she had ignored his presence, and continued dancing with her friends.

"Forgive me now, please Rahul. Come on, don't be a kid now."

Hari was watching all this from the sidelines, feeling proud of the way Rahul was handling himself. He always wanted him to have such self-respect, and he was glad that he was showing it then. Little did he know that Rahul's heart was shouting inside him, pleading him to forgive her. *Come on, forgive her. Look at her innocence. She is speaking the truth. She cares for you;* his heart pleaded with him.

"Please, please, please...." Shreya continued, asking for forgiveness.

Not able to take it any longer, he pushed back his chair, got up and ran towards the washroom.

His abrupt and violent gesture worried Shreya. She glanced towards Hari for guidance. Hari closed both his eyes momentarily, tilting his head, as a signal that she shouldn't worry about him.

Leaning over the washbasin, Rahul opened the tap in full flow and began washing his eyes.

He was not feeling sleepy, and neither were his eyes aching; his heart was. He tried to conceal from himself the water that streamed down from his eyes with the water that went into his eyes. He wanted to tell her how much he had missed her the entire night and how eagerly he wanted to forgive her from the first moment that she said sorry.

After spending a good ten minutes in the washroom, he came out looking fresh. He gave Hari a quick wink and started laughing uncontrollably. Hari joined him in his laughing and they exchanged high-fives.

"What happened?" You guys are crazy or what?" Shreya said, perplexed at the sudden change in Rahul's behaviour.

"You thought I was really serious about all that, right?" Rahul said, in a mocking tone, laughing all the while.

"You mean you were playing a prank on me?"

"You bet."

"I would kill you both. You know how scared I was when you abruptly got up and went to the washroom?"

"Hahaha….heheheh" they continued laughing in unison.

She failed to pick up the grief behind that laughter. And that's what Rahul wanted. That was the only way he could have made things come back to normal after accidentally letting her know his feelings. His impromptu plan worked perfectly.

The Offsite

Riya, Rahul, Shreya and Hari entered the office after having lunch at Pizza Hut, which was just two blocks away from office. They saw the project manager, Varsha, standing in the bay, looking around the floor, and hurried to their seats.

"Hey Shreya, I was waiting for you guys," Varsha said, as the four of them stood in the bar, encircling her.

"Oh, sorry we came a little late from lunch", Shreya said.

"No issues. Ok. I just wanted to announce that we are going to Ranikhet next weekend, that is, Friday, to have some fun. All of you who are interested can join. We would be leaving at around 11 p.m. from the office itself.

"That's cool. Is the trip meant for our department only or others too?" Riya asked excitedly.

"Our department and the B2B sales department. Approximately twenty people, if all of them decide to come", Varsha replied.

"We are coming for sure," Riya said, smiling at the other three, as if expecting a sure shot yes. The three nodded in turn.

With that exciting news, it was time for everybody to get chatting and make plans on what all to take to the trip. Each one started preparing their own list – music, books, shoes, clothes, cameras – there was a noticeable buzz in the bay and that made them the envy of others on the floor. Shreya prepared her own list for shopping.

"Rahul, would you mind giving me company for some shopping? I need to buy some books and CDs for the trip," she said, sheepishly, afraid that he might refuse.

He yet again put his ego aside and decided to help her with the shopping.

Shut up, you idiot. Can't you see how desperately she needs my help? She is all alone. He shouted out loud in response to his ego, which was stopping him from committing the mistake he had done in the past.

The next three days, Rahul and Shreya went shopping after office. He had no clue which music was good, or which was the latest chartbuster; but he enjoyed her company, while she made her choices, occasionally asking for his opinion. Her being close to him mattered to him the most. The moments spent shopping with her, holding her bags, touching her accidentally, she clutching his arm tightly while crossing the road, were heaven to him and he did not want to leave heaven.

The day of the departure arrived. Before leaving office at 6:00 p.m., she reminded him for picking her up from her place at 9 o'clock. She had told him that she didn't feel safe driving alone after 9 and Rahul was more than willing to do it for her. She said her goodbyes and left for her place, while Rahul remained in the office, along with Hari, as they had to take care of an important assignment. Riya left too, excited to be a part of the trip, and promised to see them a few hours later.

Rahul and Hari left office at 7:30, after finishing off an important chunk of the assignment. Rahul had to meet a client at 8:30, so they decided that they would go to Hari's place, freshen up, pick up their already packed bags, have a short meeting with the client, and then pick up Shreya from her place at 9.

Rahul had brought his bags to Hari's place overnight, so that he won't have to go to his room. They reached Hari's room at 8, quickly freshened up, picked up their bags, and left for the meeting with the client. Just as they were about to sit in the car, Rahul's phone buzzed. It was Shreya.

"Hey, me coming. You stay ready. We will pick you up," Rahul said, the moment he picked up her call.

"Rahul...." she started crying, "Rahul, I am not feeling well. I won't be able to come along. You guys please carry on," she said, onerously.

Rahul immediately put the phone down and asked Hari to drive as fast as possible to Shreya's place.

"But the client?" Hari asked him for almost flooring the pedal.

"I don't care. She is crying. Something is wrong," Rahul shouted, almost coming to tears himself. They covered the half an hour's distance to her place in 15 minutes. Rahul ran upstairs, not bothering to wait for the lift to arrive, even thought her apartment was on the eighth floor, while Hari parked the car in the parking lot for visitors.

He knocked on the door.

He could hear footsteps approaching the door and waited for her to open it.

She was still wearing the same pink dress she had worn to office earlier in the day. He could see her dried tears on her cheeks and the faint lines that the wiping off had left.

She immediately lay down on bed after opening the door, holding her stomach and grimacing in pain.

"What happened? You don't look alright."

"My stomach is paining like hell. I won't be able to go. Please, you guys go. Don't spoil the fun because of me."

"But who will take care of you here? You are alone."

"I'll be okay. Don't worry about me."

"No. Either you are coming with us or I am staying back too. It's dangerous to leave you alone in such a condition. At least at the camp, we would be there to take care of you. Come on, get up. I will pack your bags. Just tell me what all to put in."

She smiled at his sweet gesture and decided not to protest any further. She went to the washroom and changed into a loose fitting tee and a casual, red pair of pyjamas, along with green flip flops to go with it.

Rahul helped her pack in all the things that were strewn around the place. He couldn't help but glance at her every now and then. He could feel the beauty of her soul, and the beauty of her physical self even in that simple outfit. Her presence was like a magnet to him, which kept tugging at his heart's strings relentlessly. They quickly packed the stuff, locked the doors, and went down to the ground floor, where Hari was waiting for them.

She was feeling a little better, but was still holding onto her stomach in obvious pain.

"Hey, you okay?" Hari asked, concerned.

"Yeah."

"Okay. Both of you sit at the back. It's more comfortable back there," Hari said, asking them to sit at the back seat of the car.

Hari drove the car cautiously avoiding the potholes and the speed breakers that came in the way. He was conscious of Shreya's condition and took every possible measure to bring her minimum possible discomfort on the way to the pick up point.

They reached the pick up point at 10 o' clock sharp, but there was no sign of anybody around. Hari parked the car in the parking lot, which was empty, except for one black sedan, which had a driver sleeping inside it. It was humid outside, so they decided to stay in the car with the air conditioner switched on, until people start to arrive.

"God damn it. There is no sign of anybody around here. I hope they are not playing a prank on us", Rahul said, concerned at seeing nobody at the designated time.

"Nopes, we have company," Shreya said, pointing towards a female figure approaching the office complex. It was Riya. Dressed in a green t-shirt and black cargos, she looked her usual cheerful self.

The three of them got down from the car and locked it. Riya gave each of them a hug, while asking them the reason for the absence of the bus that was supposed to be there at 10.

"Where is the bus?" Did somebody contact Miss Varsha?" she asked.

"Nopes," came the prompt response from Rahul.

"Then contact her and ask her where the bus is, and where is she."

"Chill babes. She would come, and the bus would too. See. People have started arriving already," Rahul replied, and pointed to a group of four people who were coming in a car to the office. They were not from their team.

"They must be from the B2B sales team," Shreya guessed.

"Yeah."

They indulged in some casual chit chat, discussing about everything they would do at Ranikhet and how it was going to be the best trip ever. They got so engrossed in the conversation that they didn't realise it was almost 11:30, and the bus had already arrived. Most of the seats were already taken, barring a few at the back.

They quickly hopped on the bus, and could see Miss Varsha sitting on the first seat of the bus, already engrossed in a book. They decided not to interrupt her and passed on without greeting her.

They could see most of their teammates, some of them chatting spiritedly with each other, while others waiting casually for the journey to begin. Riya purposely kept Hari by her side and the two grabbed the seats at the end of the bus. She wanted to give Rahul the chance to spend the journey with Shreya. Shreya and Rahul took their seats together, just ahead of Riya, Shreya sitting on the window seat while Rahul took the adjoining one. Rahul got hold of her bag and dumped it in the overhead compartment, and he did the same for Riya, Hari and himself.

"Thanks," said Shreya.

It's another ten minutes before the bus started to the onwards journey of Ranikhet. A few people had already slept by that time, while the others were busy chatting and humming songs. Riya was busy talking to Hari, asking him about his family and his life in general.

"So you don't have any brother or sister?" she asked Hari.

"No."

"Okay."

Shreya started reading a book she had brought along. It was a murder mystery written by Sidney Sheldon. She reclined her seat a bit, supported both her knees on the back of the front seat, crossed her feet and started turning the pages.

Seeing her sitting in such a relaxed manner aroused strong feelings in Rahul. He wanted to hug her tight, and spend the rest of the night telling her how much he cherished that moment.

Half an hour into the journey, everybody was fast asleep, while Shreya was busy reading the book. Suddenly, she clasped the side of her stomach with both her hands and started crying. The book she was reading fell down, as she grimaced in pain. The noise of sobbing woke up Rahul, who immediately got up from his seat and asked her to lie down, with her legs stretched.

With her head by the window seat and her legs on the other, she lay down, her hands still by her stomach, but not clenched tightly. She dozed off to sleep within a couple of minutes of lying down, while Rahul stood by her side, watching her innocence with the admiration of a star struck fan.

He was tired himself but didn't feel any inclination to sit down. He was happy to see her sleeping peacefully. A smile broke across his face as he watched her sleeping with the innocence of a baby.

Always keep her healthy and happy. Please, it is my humble request. He prayed to God.

It was almost an hour since she went to sleep, when she woke up because of the sudden jerk of the bus. The driver had suddenly applied the brakes to prevent the dog, which had suddenly come in front, from getting run over. Shreya opened her eyes and saw Rahul standing in front of her.

"How are you now?" he asked.

"Better. You were standing all this while?"

She didn't get an answer. Rahul smiled and looked away towards Hari and Riya, who were awake, too. He didn't want her to feel guilty about making him stand. He didn't want her to feel as if she had done something wrong; because she hadn't....

"Come sit," she said, as she got up and sat on the seat by the window, leaving the other one vacant for Rahul to sit on.

"Lie down, else your stomach would pain again", Rahul said, ignoring his own discomfort after standing for more than an hour at a stretch.

"Either you are sitting, or I am also standing up," she said, in a kiddish tone.

"Okay," he said, smiling at her gesture and sat down beside her. "You can keep your feet on my lap and lie down if you want to," he said, noticing the strain on her face while she was sitting.

"Thanks," she replied gleefully and got back to her previous position – head by the window and her legs in Rahul's lap.

Rahul could not sleep the entire night. The weight of her legs was too much for his lanky frame to bear, but he bore it without showing any signs of uneasiness. He was happy that she was sleeping peacefully, and that is what mattered to him the most.

The bus reached Ranikhet at eleven in the morning. Everybody got down with their luggage and rushed straight inside the cottage, which was exclusively booked for them. Rahul carried his own luggage along with Shreya's, while she walked along his side to the cottage. Hari and Riya followed them.

Shreya and Riya picked up the room on the far end of the corridor, on the first floor, while Rahul and Hari stayed in the room next to them, which was the only one left.

"It looks beautiful, isn't it?" Riya said, looking at the view of the mountains as she opened the curtains.

"Yeah," Shreya replied, lying down on bed, her arms spread wide and her legs bent at the knees.

"I am going off to sleep."

"Me too," Riya said.

Most of the people went to sleep, with plans of going on an excursion late in the evening, and exploring the hill station. Hari and Rahul went off to sleep, too.

ooo

Riya unpacked her bag and took out a tee and a pair of jeans to change into. They were going on a shopping trip to the nearby market.

"Hey, aren't you coming with us?" Riya asked Shreya, who was still lying on bed, with her eyes open.

"No, I don't think I would be able to go today. It's still paining. I would take rest. You people go and enjoy," she said, with a half-hearted smile.

"Okay. Take care. But you are coming to the bonfire at night. I won't listen to any excuses then," Riya said, going to the washroom to change her clothes.

Dressed in a black t-shirt and matching jeans and shoes, Rahul barged into Shreya's room, excited, "Why are you not ready till now? Come on, we will be late," he said, almost grabbing her arm and forcing her to get up.

"I can't go. It's still paining. You people go ahead. I will join you at the bonfire tonight."

"No ways. We can't leave you alone in such a condition. I'll stay with you," he said, and came and sat next to her.

"I will be fine, trust me. You should go. You don't have to miss out on the fun because of me," she urged Rahul.

"No arguments. I am staying with you. Our team leader is more important to us than fun," he said, consciously speaking as if he was saying this on behalf of the whole team so as not to let her feel that he was making a sacrifice for her.

When it came to her, it wasn't sacrifice for him. He was looking forward to go shopping with the group, but her health was far more important to him. Spending time with her was a million times more precious to him than an outing with the group in the peaceful environment of the hills which he loved.

"Hey dumbo, come, let's go," Riya said, as she came out of the washroom, dressed in a fresh pair of clothes.

"No, I am staying with her. You carry on. Take Hari along. He is in his room."

"You sure?"

"Yes."

"Okay, bye, see you later," she said and went out of the room.

"Do you want tea or coffee?" Rahul asked Shreya.

"No, thanks."

Rahul opened the curtains of the room and was mesmerised by the view outside. The sun was setting down, which gave the sky an orangish hue. The orange of the sky and the green of the mountain had a soothing effect on his senses.

"Wow, Shreya, look...."

She had gone to sleep. He quietly closed the curtains and came and sat on the chair kept by the side of the bed. He picked up a book which was kept on the table and began flipping through its pages; but his complete attention was towards her.

He tried hard to concentrate on what the author wanted to convey with his words, but her purity was too strong a magnetic force for him to stay away from.

He wanted to kiss her, but not in a lustful manner. He wanted to take her in his arms, but only to feel the magic of her soul. He wanted to lie by her side only to let her know how special she was. He could not feel any other emotions apart from love, even though he knew he was in a position which most guys would give their right arm for – in the room of a nubile woman, all alone with her.

ooo

It was almost two hours before the group came back from their shopping trip. Most of them were empty-handed, except Riya, who had three bags full of small souvenirs and other items which she had bought. Riya and Hari came straight to Shreya's room, excited at their first trip of the town. Riya could not stop chirping about their shopping experience and Hari genuinely looked happy with her blabbering.

Their chatting woke up Shreya, who was sleeping until then. Rubbing her eyes and putting off the blanket which was wrapped around her body, she said, groggily, "Hey guys, you are back. How was the shopping?"

"Good. Fantastic! How are you now?" Riya butted in, not giving Hari a chance to speak.

"I am good. I guess I would be able to attend the bonfire," Shreya replied with a glance towards Rahul and smiled. It was a gesture common among humans when saying thank you; and for Rahul, it meant the world. He was happy that Shreya appreciated his gesture, and he took it as a step towards more closeness between them.

"Great. Then get ready in half an hour. It's almost 8. The bonfire starts at 9, and there is loads of food, and a DJ as well," Riya said excitedly.

"Okay, I will be ready by then," Shreya replied, reciprocating the excitement.

Rahul went to his room along with Hari, leaving the two girls behind to get ready for the bonfire.

"So dude, you and Shreya alone in one room, huh. What's up?" Hari said in a teasing manner.

"Shut up! You filthy head! I was just there to take care of her. Thank goodness she is all right now."

"Hmm ... and all because of you. You are great man. I mean if she had done all those things to me, I would have left her long ago. But you are great. Kudos to you."

"What things?" She didn't do anything wrong. She did what people would do in her situation. We can't expect everybody to reciprocate our feelings quickly. She is good, and I know it", Rahul replied, trying hard to defend her. In his conscience, he knew what she had done was wrong, but he had forgiven her for that. His love for her was stronger than any other emotion that he felt.

"Yeah, but still...."

"Still what?" Rahul interrupted, "Didn't you see how thankful she was to me for staying back? That's the sign of a good person."

"Okay, chill. You win. Get ready for the bonfire. It's time to *chiggy wiggy*."

"Absolutely," Rahul replied, excitedly. He was looking forward to the bonfire and the DJ night as he would have the chance to ask Shreya for a dance. He wasn't a great dancer, but the thought of dancing close to her made him giddy and feverish. He quickly had a hot shower and changed into a casual pair of short shirt and a fitting pair of jeans. He combed his hair to perfection, had a good look in the mirror and shouted, "Hari, are you going to get ready today or not?" Hari was in the washroom for the past twenty minutes, yodelling a Boney M number.

"Five more minutes," Hari shouted back.

"Okay. I am going to the girls' room to see if they are ready. Put everything in the locker and lock the room once you come out."

"Sure."

Rahul knocked on the girls' door, and it was immediately opened by Riya.

"Hi. You are looking cute," Rahul said.

"Thanks", she replied. She was wearing a red knee length skirt and a matching top, along with a muffler. And then he was almost mesmerised looking at the person right next to Riya. It was Shreya, looking gorgeous in a black top.

"Hi Shreya! How are you feeling now? By the way, you are looking gorgeous!" He said.

"Thanks Rahul", Shreya replied. The happiness of someone praising her was quite evident on her face. She completely ignored the other question. Everyone walked down to the party lawn, and Shreya was soon lost in the crowd completely ignoring the support and presence of Rahul. Everyone was enjoying the party talking to their friends while Rahul was quietly standing at a corner sipping his drink.

"Hey Rahul! Come dance no!" Riya asked him.

"No Riya. I don't know dancing. I am fine here. You guys carry on," he said smiling, trying hard to let his loneliness inside him creep up.

"Leave him Riya! He is such a boring person. I don't understand that why people come to parties when they can't even enjoy it." It was Shreya's voice from the far end. The same Shreya, for whom he cared for, by ignoring his team excursions, was now back to her usual self once she was feeling a bit better. Listening to her words, Rahul just managed to smile.

Everyone again got busy in the party trying to put a fake smile on their empty and hollow faces.

"Ladies and Gentlemen, finish off your dinner quickly. I am your DJ for the night. See you all on the dance floor soon." The DJ announced. Soon after, everyone was busy shaking their legs on the floor. But Rahul's eyes were still glued towards Shreya, who was looking absolutely stunning and distinct within the crowd. He saw her and waved his hands. She gave him a smile, and asked him to come over.

'Come on Rahul! This is your chance to let her know your feelings'. His inner voice said. Quiet enthralled by her invitation, he stepped forward, completely forgetting the recent incident.

Suddenly his steps were taken aback, as he realised she was still waving her hands in the same direction. He moved back in the direction and saw the French guy John waving his hands back at her. Before he could understand the situation, John moved towards Shreya and offered her a dance. Soon both were engrossed within each other, while all the other colleagues were encouraging both of them for the extremely sensual dance.

Rahul could not bear the cheering anymore, and clutched the rose as hard as possible which he picked very enthusiastically to present to Shreya before the dance. It quickly fell out from his hand leaving his hand blood stained by the thorns. Hari noticed it first and came running towards him, quickly wrapping his handkerchief around his hand.

"You asshole, can't you see it's hurting you!" Hari almost yelled at him. Though he managed to see the outer bruises, but failed to pick an even larger wound which was deep within Rahul, completely invisible to anyone. Two tiny drops of tears rolled down his eyes. He immediately left the party and did not remember when he was fast asleep.

The next day, everyone started packing their bags. Rahul as usual helped Shreya in her packing. Until now they had not spoken a single word since last night.

"Hey Rahul! Why did you leave yesterday in the middle of the party? You were talking to your girlfriend! Hmm…." Shreya asked. Rahul kept quiet and just smiled.

'How could he tell her the underlying pain which he went through last night? Can't she understand that?' He thought to himself. Everyone hopped inside the bus. This time Shreya had taken the seat next to John completely ignoring the presence of Rahul. Rahul and Hari sat together quietly, and Hari just managed to give a pat on his shoulders. Even he was falling short of words at that moment.

OOO

It was three days after everyone came back from the offsite. Rahul was in his bed, but his mind was still wandering around Shreya's thoughts.

I have got to tell her my feelings. I trust my universe and I know the universe would never let me down. He made the resolve to propose her while lying in bed and thinking about her. He rehearsed his lines mentally but could not decide on the final version he would use.

Shreya, I want to say something. We have been friends for quite some time now but the truth is, I see you more than just a friend. I love you and I want to spend the rest of my life with you. Another one went, *I want to say something Shreya. I love you.* Still another one was phrased, *Shreya, the moment I saw you on the first day of office, I fell in love with you. I want to spend the rest of my life with you....*

His mind kept coming up with new lines every minute until he fell asleep.

ooo

He was typing on his computer screen but his mind was thinking about the moment he would tell Shreya his feelings. He had planned that he would ask her out for a coffee in the evening, and there were still four hours to go for the tea break. The four hours felt like an eternity to him. His mind raced to all sorts of reactions his actions would trigger in her – delight, anger, nonchalance, empathy, disgust and every conceivable human emotion.

He rejected all of those and concentrated on the Universe he so firmly believed in. He was sure he would get a positive response. He had started getting the vibes from her in the past few days which made him feel so. Her clutching his arm while crossing the road, her frequent shopping trips with him, her sharing her feelings with him....he took all that as a sign from the universe that she liked him.

After waiting for all day long for the moment to come, it finally arrived. It was five in the evening and it was time for the tea break.

"Hey Shreya, let's go for a coffee downstairs to CCD," he said, jittery from within.

"Okay, Ri…."

He quickly whisked her away before she could shout out Riya and Hari's name. He did not want anybody to be around while he opened his heart to her. But God had other plans for him.

They took the corner table and ordered a cappuccino each.

"Why didn't you call Riya and Hari?"

"Because I wanted to talk to you alone."

"Why?" she asked with an expression that seemed as if she knew what was coming. Rahul saw that and it made him even more jittery.

"Shreya … actually, I just…."

Someone's presence on his right interrupted his statement. He glanced upwards and saw Mike standing there.

"Hi Shreya, how are you?" Mike asked.

Bastard! What does he want from her? Can't she see his devious smile? Can't she look beyond her fake charm and figure out his real intentions? Rahul sulked quietly while Shreya offered Mike a chair.

"So, how is it going?"

"It's going great. You tell me, what's up with you? Oh, by the way, this is Rahul, my colleague and a friend, and Rahul, this is Mike," she said.

"Hi," Rahul replied, almost rudely, choosing not to shake his extended arm.

Sensing that his purpose was lost and angry at her for letting Mike budge in his private moments with her, he decided to leave.

He got up and answered Shreya's quizzical expression, "It just struck me. I have to complete a very important task that has been pending for long," and added, "You enjoy your coffee with Mike," speaking the last part in concealed sarcasm that only he could comprehend.

He decided he would shoot her a mail first and wait for her response instead of a face-to-face conversation.

I would write her an e-mail just before leaving. I want to give her time to think about it. She would have the whole night.

Proposal and the Heartbreak Again

It's quarter to seven when he decides to write her the proposal e-mail. He wrote about the feelings she aroused in him the first time he saw her, how she is her first and last love and how he wants to spend the rest of the life with her. He tried his best to convey the same feelings he felt when he looked at her, when he thought about her, when he talked to her….

It read –

Hi Miss Makeup,

I was intended to write you this mail much before. But, you are so busy with your own work that it took me long to convey the same.

I wanted to tell you about all this, in person. I was trying hard to meet you for some time, since last 2-3 days, but what a poor chap I am. You didn't have time.

May be after this mail, you will not be able to talk with me freely, like before. May be you will be in a state of shock. But, for me, it was quite much necessary to tell you everything.

I don't know what you think about me. I also don't know where life will take us in future, but one thing is for sure that you will always remain the most important person, whom I simply will not forget ever in my life throughout.

I know you are not surprised by the line, as you might have already sensed it long before. But, I will feel guilty about it whole of my life, that I didn't let you know this in person.

I know I am no where, if I try comparing myself with you. I do accept this bitter and honest fact. But, I simply couldn't help but fall for you, your beauty, your attitude, your sweetness, and to top it all your precious moments being with me. Perhaps the bonding was getting stronger day-by-day.

I have kept all your memories, and the moments of our togetherness with myself, which will keep on tickling me whenever I think about them. Sorry for stealing your memories with me, but these will always be mine!

Few moments which I will always remember:

a. Our first out-of-the-office interaction in Archie's. All thanks to Prerna's birthday for that. Otherwise we would have been just like two people knowing each other by name. That's it. But, it was that interaction, which made me think, that there is also a different, sweet, and charming 'Shreya' hidden behind the quiet and arrogant 'Shreya' in the office.

b. Our first movie together. Remember the horror movie we went to see together. Thereafter, we went to see few more movies together. That was the time, when I just started liking your company. Don't know, whether you understood then or not..

c. Being with you throughout the offsite. At times, I felt like cuddling/hugging you to let you forget all your pain. But, I was always in a sense of dilemma, what if you take it otherwise, which was not my intention at all. I tried my best to take care of you. I always tried to be there, whenever you needed me.

d. At times, during the bus journey, I used to look back at you and your sweetness again and again. In fact, this was the time when I realised that I am seriously in love, and perhaps you are the perfect person, as you are the most adorable kid whom I would want to take care of and act as the best possible caretaker forever in my life, of course by getting married with this sweet princess.

Though I should not say it, but it's actually the offsite, which brought my dormant feelings for you to a prominent note.

Throughout my life, I think I have hardly broken a single heart, but my heart after many setbacks, has become almost like a brittle stone. It seems very hard from outside, facing every thing so easily, but all it needs is a sheer touch to be broken into pieces. May be, it is just because I always thought that all we need is a good heart, good soul, and a bonding between each other to have a successful relationship. But, almost all the times, that initial attraction overshadows all the goodness. But you know life is the biggest faculty which teaches us a new lesson everyday, by our own experiences.

And I sincerely believe it's you with whom I would like to spend my whole life. I don't know how much one can do for you. I don't say, I will die for you, but definitely, I will always try to keep you happy throughout.

Even if you say no, I will somehow try to accept it. I may be just the ordinary boy next door, but, I am what I am, and I will always be the same. I'll always try to invade through your thoughts.

But, nevertheless, all I want is your happiness. Even if it's a no, please at least be in touch with me always. Life goes on. I will just hope that we meet again at some point of time in our life, and hopefully you don't regret your earlier decision then.

So, in a nutshell, what I could not say on your face ever is that I love you, and wish to spend the rest of my life with you. Did you also feel the same for me? Please let me know!

Love You Always.

And then he decided to leave. He didn't tell Hari about it; he was too preoccupied visualising her reactions to tell anybody about it. They passed their journey in silence. Rahul didn't have dinner and went straight to bed; his apprehensions about the day to come were taking control over his natural wants. He eagerly waited for the sun to rise; not because he was sure of her affirmative answer, but because he wished for.

Next morning, he got up full of anxious excitement. He didn't feel like having breakfast. He was feeling too giddy to put anything in his mouth. He got dressed casually, unaware that the shirt he was wearing was not ironed. He forgot his watch on the table, locked the door and went outside to the main gate where Hari was already waiting for him in his car.

When they reached office, Shreya was already there working on her system, even though it was still not 10. Rahul tried reading her expressions from a distance but there were none. Shreya greeted both of them, and Rahul's heart skipped a beat as she said hi. He tried making sense of the tone of her voice but failed.

She must have read the e-mail by now. Why isn't she responding? She greeted me normally. Does it mean that ... wow, that really means ... I knew it; I knew you are always there with me. He thought, making conjectures from her neutral behaviour and thanking God for it. He waited eagerly for Shreya to say something directly as he settled down on his chair. She continued working, almost oblivious of his presence.

It was not before lunchtime that Shreya called him and said, "Rahul, let's have lunch someplace today. Just you and me!" The last part of the sentence evoked a thrilling excitement in Rahul. He was sure of the response from her and prepared mentally in all sorts of way to present the ring to her that he had bought a couple of days back. It was a gold ring, with a tiny diamond on top. The ring was not expensive, but to Rahul, it was priceless. It was to be the symbol of victory of love for him.

They went to Pizza Hut, which was two blocks away from office. Rahul ordered a medium thin crust pizza with extra cheese for the two of them and they both settled into their chairs in a corner. The restaurant had plenty of empty chairs, although it was lunch hour.

"Rahul, I need to talk to you," she said, with a straight face.

"I know. Tell me," Rahul replied, with a broad smile—and then his smile vanished.

"Rahul, the thing is ... you are a very good person. You are one of my very good friends. But I don't love you. I can't ever love you. You are not the kind of person I am looking for to spend the rest of my life with. You are good but...." she paused, reading the sorrow on his face.

But what? You need a good-looking person who has loads of money, who is a status symbol for you while making your public appearances, even if he lusts after your physical beauty? That's what you want, right? His disappointment spoke inside him and he restrained himself from blurting it out. She didn't apologise for her response and neither did she say anything after that. She kept looking at him.

He clutched the ring inside his pocket and got up to leave. She didn't stop him.

○○○

Two days passed by since she rejected him. *I know I would get her. I have heard stories about love winning at the end, and I know they are true. I still believe in You and I know You will not let me down.*

He still believed his love would win and he was sure of his belief. It was his belief that made him sit next to her everyday and continue working the way he used to. Though he sat next to her everyday, but he could feel the distance grow between them. The distance was not physical; the aloofness of Shreya after that episode was palpable to him, but his belief in love gave him strength to not leave the city and go away.

And his belief triumphed. It was Thursday, and it was a normal working day for him until she asked him to accompany her on a shopping trip. It was almost a month since they had gone out together; that small incidence was a big victory for his belief.

"Of course, let's go," he agreed immediately. His sister had called him the same day many a time to take her for her doctor's appointment. He decided to go to her sister's place in Delhi the next week. Love meant more to him than blood.

Both decided to leave after lunchtime and they went to the nearby mall. Shreya had to buy some clothes for herself. Rahul didn't care the reason behind the shopping. He just wanted to be close to her and wanted her to behave normally with him; the way she did before he proposed her. Little did he know the actual reason behind the shopping.

"Hey, how is this sari?" Shreya asked, showing him a fuchsia coloured embellished sari.

"You would wear a sari? Are you kidding?" he said, in a perplexed mocking tone.

"Yeah, why not."

"It looks good, but…."

"But what? You think I can't carry it off? Is that what you mean?"

"No … it's not that. I mean, a sari is worn on a family function or something of that sort," he said, apprehensively.

"Yeah, so, I'm….ouch, God … it's happening again", she clutched her stomach and sat down on the floor, writhing in acute pain.

OOO

"You will be alright, don't worry," Rahul said, driving as fast as he could to take her to the hospital. He had taken the help of a passerby in the mall to take Shreya to the car. He held her hand while he took control of the steering wheel with one hand. Though he was more nervous than Shreya, he pretended himself to be calm and silently hoped for her well-being, as he concentrated on the road ahead, swerving with caution to reach the hospital as early as he could.

"She's alright now. I've given her the medicines. She needs to take rest for at least a week," the doctor said.

"Thanks doc," Rahul replied.

He helped her get back to the car and drove back to her place. He was thankful that she was alright. He didn't remember anything about their conversation in the mall and the fact that she was in the middle of a sentence when she experienced the pain. He was too preoccupied with forbidding thoughts of her health to think of anything else.

He stopped the car in front of the gates and waited for her to get down.

"You alright? Should I leave you upstairs?" He asked.

"Yeah, I'm perfect. Thanks."

"Rahul!"

"Yeah," he replied, surprised at the unexpected tender tone of her voice.

She hugged him tightly. "I don't know what this relationship is. But it is definitely one that I will cherish for a long time to come. Thank you so much for being with me," she said.

He was too overwhelmed with this gesture to speak anything. He gazed as she went upstairs. He started the car and went back home, confused at how to response to the situation. He didn't want to read into the situation, but he couldn't help himself. He couldn't help but think of it as another victory of his love. He was sure sooner or later, he would get her.

○○○

"Hello Uncle, how are you?" said Rahul, as he made his way through some known and unknown faces towards the groom's seat. It was his cousin, Utsav's marriage, who was getting hooked to his college sweetheart Megha. *How lucky Utsav is. He is getting married to the one he has always loved. I wish I was lucky too.*

"Oh, hi Aunty, you are looking gorgeous," said Rahul as Utsav's mom broke his train of thoughts.

"Thank you so much. Rahul, the gifts for the guests have not arrived. Could you please check why has the guy not reached yet? There is so much to do, I hope everything goes as planned," said Utsav's mom.

"Don't worry aunty; I will take care of everything. Relax." And with that, Rahul was away, dialling the number of the gifts' guy frantically on his mobile, trying to get in touch with him.

In his black tuxedo, gelled hair and shining black shoes, he was looking nothing short of dapper.

His long strides and upright gait told everything about his confidence today, which was sky high, something which was a rarity.

If only Shreya could see me so well-dressed, maybe she would propose me herself, thought Rahul, with a broad grin on his face. *Wow, what a moment it would be when that happens.*

Every night in my dreams
I see you, I feel you
That is how I know you go on
Far across the distance
And spaces between us
You have come to show you go on....

It was his cell phone ringing. *Shreya calling* displayed the illuminated screen of the mobile.

Shreya! Why is she calling me? Has something happened to her? Is she in some sort of difficulty? I hope she is okay. Maybe she is just calling to say hi. But she has never done that before.

"Hi Shreya!" spoke Rahul, anxious and excited at the same time.

"Hi Rahul, how are you?" said Shreya. Those words sounded to Rahul the same way they would sound to a deaf person who has just got back his ability to hear – sweet but mystical.

Shreya always evoked the same feelings in him. It was not the first time they were talking on phone but Rahul always went through this anxiety while talking to her, like a school kid talking on the phone for the first time.

"I am good Shreya, you tell me, how are you?" said Rahul, slowly regaining his self composure.

"I am good too Rahul. I need a small favour from you. There are a few friends coming to my place for a party and there is loads of work to do. But I do not have anybody to help me out with the preparations. Even Riya is out of reach today. Could you please come to my place to lend me a hand? I really need you, else I am screwed. Please!"

I really need you. Those four words spun like a tornado in his subconscious. It was a dream he had long cherished. He had spent sleepless nights imagining her saying exactly that – *I really need you.* It was a heady feeling for him. Of course, she meant it in a different sense altogether but it was a perfect opportunity for him to show her how much he cared for her.

"Come on Shreya, no need to say please. Of course I will be there. After all, what are friends meant for! Don't worry, chill," said Rahul, forgetting that he had a wedding to attend to, forgetting that he had just made a promise to his aunt that he would take care of things, forgetting that it was his social duty to be there when his cousin exchanges vows with his beloved. Everything was secondary to him because Shreya needed him, his love needed him.

"Thank you so much Rahul, you are such a sweetheart. But please be here in half an hour as people would start arriving in a couple of hours and we have loads to do. See you in thirty", and with that Shreya hung up.

We have loads to do. WE! Is it another signal from the universe that finally my love is winning? He thought, but his apprehensions remained. He decided he would help Shreya with the preparation and leave the scene before the party started. He didn't want to spoil her fun by staying too long.

Juggling with his train of thoughts, he reached Shreya's place 45 minutes after he received her call. After parking his car, he quickly ran upstairs without even waiting for the lift. Shreya was eagerly waiting for him.

"Hey Rahul! Thanks a ton. It's only you whom I can rely on such circumstances. Hope you didn't have anything important to do," she asked.

"No No! Nothing so important", he smiled and said quickly, completely hiding the fact about his cousin's wedding back home.

Both were soon busy arranging for the party. Rahul helped her in peeling the onion, cooking the delicious chicken, preparing the tables, etc. Suddenly the door bell rang.

"Rahul, probably my friends have come. Could you please open the door? My hands are dirty," Shreya shouted from the kitchen.

He opened the door and found two unknown faces standing at the door. Both of them also got confused for a while seeing Rahul opening the door.

"Umm....I am Ved and she is Vinita, her cousins. Is Shreya's inside?" one of them managed to ask still unsure about the answer.

"Yeah, please come inside. By the way, I am Rahul," he paused for a while and continued, "Shreya's office colleague." He extended his hands for a handshake which was responded back with the same intensity.

"Hey guys, I was waiting for you since long. By the way, did you meet my colleague Rahul. Had he not been there I would have been helpless arranging all this," she said excitedly.

Ved handed her the gift and said, "Best of luck for your future endeavours. Hope you will soon get accustomed to Bangalore and its climate."

'Bangalore!!! It means she is leaving Gurgaon. But she did not even tell me about it,' he said to himself.

"Shreya! You are going to Bangalore? Congrats yar, you did not even tell me about this. By the way which firm are you going to join?" he asked.

"He he," both Ved and Vinita laughed in unison, with Shreya joining them too with just a smile. "Shreya you did not tell him or what. Well, Shreya is getting married after a month and we are here to celebrate the news," Ved said.

Rahul stood still for a while, frozen at his place. "Hey Rahul, are you alright? What have you started thinking now?" Ved caught him by his shoulders.

"Umm, nothing. Sorry," Rahul said.

The next few hours, Shreya was busy talking about her would be husband, what he does, etc. Rahul was least interested in these now. All he wanted desperately was to get back to his cousin's marriage ceremony.

The party was over at 1 in the midnight and both Ved and Vinita left. While Shreya expected that Rahul will also leave, to her surprise he climbed back the stairs along with her. Both reached to her flat and were silent for a few minutes.

"Sorry, I was about to tell you all this, but did not get the courage to break your heart. You know you are such a sweet person, and anyone will be fortunate spending her life with you," she said.

'Huh, anyone then why not you?' he thought.

For next hour Rahul was busy with Shreya in cleaning up the mess. It was 2 when everything was cleaned, and Shreya was all tired.

"I am very much tired now. Rahul, can you please do me a favour? Put this balm on my head," she asked him for a favour.

Rahul did not answer, but quietly applied the balm on her forehead and started rubbing it. Shreya was slowly getting aroused and Rahul was aware of the situation.

Shreya had closed her eyes by then, and was waiting for Rahul to take the first step.

Rahul was aware about the delicacy of the situation, and before he could fall for the same, he gave a warm kiss on Shreya's forehead and stood. "Hey Shreya, its quite late I guess. I should leave now," he said.

Shreya looked into his eyes and she could see the amount of love Rahul had for her. She escorted him to the door, when Rahul was almost on the stairs, she called him.

"Yes, Shreya, did you say something," he asked.

Shreya came outside and embraced him tightly. "Thanks Rahul, I know you love me so much but I always see you as a good friend, and will always cherish the time spent with you."

Back home, the entire night, Rahul kept thinking about Shreya. 'She hugged me. Maybe I still have a chance. I should still keep trying to achieve my love' he did not remember when he slept thinking all this.

○○○

The next day Shreya resigned from the office leaving everyone in the office frozen for a while, as it came as a shock for everyone except Rahul. She was to leave a week after her resignation, and it was her last day today.

Rahul came to the office and realised that the office will not be the same now onwards.

'How will I be able to come here now, when you will not be there,' he thought to himself. Feeling almost at the verge of bursting out with emotions, he decided to write a farewell mail to Shreya.

It read –

Hey Sweetie,

Farewell from the office today!

Maybe from now onwards, at times, I'll just go to your seat, and then realise that there is no one there for me, whom I could tease as always!

Maybe from now onwards, at times, I'll just keep on signing-in and out of my messenger in a hope that you may come online some day!

Maybe from now onwards, I'll just call extension 1055, in a hope that you pick up the call someday and I manage to hear the long forgotten sweet voice again!

Maybe, I'll try to see the empty chair with my tearful eyes, and keep it vacant in a hope that you will again sit on it someday....

Once you will be out of the town, maybe I'll just roam around your place in a hope that someday I'll have a glimpse of you somewhere near your place....

But, my heart knows that they are just hopes, and will not turn into reality ever.

But....what to do? The poor heart still believes in miracle!

By the time, Shreya finished reading this; her eyes were almost moist with tears. For the first time, she felt how much indispensable she is from Rahul's life.

"You are such a sweetheart Rahul, I will always remember you in my life," she smiled.

ooo

Rahul, Hari and Riya were all inside Rahul's car. Rahul drove all the way to Shreya's house. Today Shreya was leaving for Bangalore with Riya and Hari. While Riya and Hari decided to accompany her for her marriage ceremony, Rahul chose not to attend her wedding. Though Shreya persuaded him several times, but he was firm on his decision.

Soon, everyone was at the airport. Rahul was quiet throughout the journey and kept looking outside, which was noticeable by everyone inside the car.

"Ok, bye Rahul, hope we meet up again at some life's crossroad. Though it would have been nice had you come along with all of us. We all would have had a fun of the lifetime then," Shreya said.

Rahul just smiled and quietly handed her the luggage. Riya and Hari waved their hands at Rahul. As the three of them were about to leave, Shreya came running to Rahul, and gave him a tight hug. Rahul could not stop his controlled emotions any longer and melted like a cloud laden with rain. Both were sobbing uncontrollably while Riya and Hari were watching it from a distance.

"I will always cherish the time spent with you. And you will remain a special person in my life throughout," she said while leaving his hand.

He saw her soon getting lost in the crowd at the airport. Again his life was colourless.

○○○

It was six months since Shreya left, and Rahul had just managed to talk to her in patches. She seemed to be happy with her new life, and Rahul was happy for her.

It is said that your past always comes back to haunt you some or the other time. It was appraisal time in the office. Rahul was engrossed in his PC when a mail popped up. It was Rahul's boss Virat who wanted to discuss Rahul's annual appraisal with him.

‘I think I will be getting a superb rating this time, as I have repeatedly done a good job. All the customers have also praised about my dedication,’ he thought to himself.

He very excitedly entered the meeting room. He looked at the Manager’s seat outside. He was busy talking to someone. ‘Cool, I have few more minutes to rehearse about the response to the praise I will be receiving today,’ he said to himself.

Suddenly he saw him disconnecting his cell phone and moving towards the meeting room. Rahul took a deep breathe and waited for him. The door opened making a loud noise and the Manager entered with a devil like smile showing all his teeth. He seemed more like a monster than a Manager to Rahul.

“Listen Rahul, You have done a good job so far as the quality of your work is concerned. But, we have received feedbacks that you don’t have a proper attitude towards work. You know in our firm it’s the dedication towards work which is given topmost priority over anything else,” he started saying in a composed tone.

“But, on what basis this has been alleged. I have always tried to give my 100% towards my work,” Rahul said in a meek tone still unable to understand the reason behind this.

“See, we have received a feedback that you went out for some personal work leaving your client meet a few months back,” he paused for a while and continued, “We don’t know what that personal work was but this reflects your preference towards your personal matters than the professional requirements. And this is NOT AT ALL ACEEPTABLE”.

He tried to scream aloud that he had to leave that day because Shreya was hospitalised. He wanted to ask whether he would have still attended the client meet had some of his own close one would have been hospitalised. But there was no point arguing with him at all, neither had he wanted to take sympathy of others. He kept quite and thought to wait for the right moment to reply.

"But it is just a one off case and you can't base a judgement about someone through this," this was all he could murmur slowly.

The Manager stared right into his eyes trying hard to beat his half-confidence and continued, "See it is not about one off case; it's about the professional traits which you have shown to the management. But as customers have shown faith in you, we have decided to give you one month to improve on this aspect. We will send you a detailed mail soon," having said this, he stood up and left the room without even waiting for Rahul's answer.

'Probably, they have pre-decided to fire me and it's a ploy for the same,' Rahul thought in his mind and came out of the room banging the door with a thud. The door kept swinging in and out for few minutes.

As soon as he reached his desk a mail popped up in his mailbox mentioning the feedback he has received recently. The mail was also copied to the VP and the HR. He almost decided to leave his job and started looking out for opportunities outside. The next few days he was busy uploading his resume on job portals.

Reunion in Bangalore

Rahul was working in his office when his phone rang. It was an unknown number but he could recognise the code; the call was from Bangalore. Half expecting it to be Shreya, he picked up the phone. "Hello," he said, and waited eagerly for a response from the other side.

"Hello, is that Rahul?" came a male voice from the other end.

"Yes, this is Rahul. Tell me."

"Rahul, I am Vinod calling from Infosys, Bangalore. Is it a good time to talk to you?"

"Yeah sure."

"Okay. Rahul, we have a job opening for you. Would you be interested in coming down to Bangalore and having a meeting with us?"

Rahul gave it a quick thought and decided to reply in the affirmative. Not because he wanted a job change, but because a chance to go to Bangalore would bring him closer to Shreya and give another opportunity to him to win her back.

"Yeah, of course, I can," he replied, enthusiastically.

They fixed up an appointment in the coming week and said their greetings.

Excited, Rahul immediately picked up his phone again and decided to call Shreya. He wanted to let her know that he would there with her to give her support in her times of difficulty. He eagerly dialled her number and impatiently waited for her to answer the call.

"Hello," came the questioning voice from the other end.

"Hi Shreya, Rahul here."

"Hi Rahul, what's up?" she replied, happily.

"Everything is fantastic. Just wanted to let you know I am coming to Bangalore. So maybe we can meet up sometime if you have some free time."

"Really? That's awesome. When are you coming?" she replied.

"This weekend. I have an interview in Infosys, and hopefully I will get the job."

"Cool. *I will wait for you.* Give me a ring whenever you arrive. We will catch up over a cup of coffee."

"Sure," and with that, he hung up. I will wait for you. Those words remained with him for the rest of the day.

○○○

It was Saturday and Rahul was super excited after having arrived in Bangalore, his hometown. He had been born and brought up in this city, but never had he been so happy to have walked the streets of Bangalore. He was about to meet his first and his last love after a very long time, and he knew the universe had bigger plans for him. *Why else would the universe bring me to Bangalore all of a sudden?* He thought to himself.

He ordered a cup of coffee while he waited for Shreya to arrive at the CCD they had decided to meet at. Rahul had called her the previous night and they had fixed up a meeting in the afternoon at the CCD at the end of MG Road.

Rahul had been sitting at the coffee shop for about 10 minutes when Shreya came through the door. Memories of office rushed back to him. The strings of love pulled at his heart again when he saw her walking towards him. She wore a sleeveless black top which hugged her body tightly, and a knee length skirt. He found the same charm in her as he did when he first saw her. Time hadn't changed her for him.

"Hi, how are you?" she said with a broad smile and extended her arm for a handshake.

Rahul gleefully took her extended arm. "Fantastic. How are you?"

"Fantastic too," she replied, looking away from him.

"Tell me the truth," he said. He could see the sorrow in her eyes.

"Nothing, it's just that ... let's order a coffee first," she said, trying to change the topic of discussion.

"Okay. Excuse me...." he said, signalling a waiter to come to their table. "Two cappuccinos please."

"Sure," the waiter said, and went away.

"Now, tell me what's bothering you?" he turned towards her and waited for her reply.

"Nothing. My life is in a mess. That's it."

"Shreya, if you have ever considered me to be a friend, please tell me what's the matter," he asked, the concern growing on his face.

"I had some problems with my husband. And then...." she paused.

"Then what?"

"I fell for the VP of the company I work in. He is a good-looking guy in his thirties. But I was a fool. I feel really guilty to have done this to my husband."

"What do you mean 'done this to my husband'? You didn't....did you?" Rahul asked, feeling ashamed to complete the sentence.

"Noooo," she shrieked, "nothing of that sort happened. But I feel guilty that I let such feelings take home in my heart. I later found out that he was married. A colleague of mine even told me that he had affairs in the past with other women too. Rahul, what if...." she broke into tears.

Understanding her guilt conscience, Rahul still hesitantly put one arm on her shoulder and said in a mellow tone, "You don't need to worry as long as I am there with you." She smiled.

OOO

He had got the job offer he had come for and had the double joy of staying at his place and close to Shreya.

He returned to Gurgaon to resign from his present firm. He went to the office after three days. There seemed to be something in the air as if the entire office was waiting for him. There was a small town hall announced where his Manager congratulated him and threw the good news. "Rahul, our customer is very happy with the work which you did for him in the past few months, and we have decided to assign you the role of the Project Manager for the client. Come forward and share your success story with the team".

Rahul moved forward holding the offer letter of Infosys in his one hand. "Thanks guys, it's no rocket science but your hard work and understanding of the client's precise requirements which matters to deliver customer delight. But in this case I would kindly request the management to decide someone else's name as the Project Manager, as I have decided to pursue the career opportunities outside the firm."

There was dead silence in the hall for a while, as no one expected such a bomb to be dropped. There were several meetings with the management for him, and they tried hard to stop him. But, Rahul was determined to leave.

Hari and Riya almost cried while he was leaving the office on his farewell day. He gave them a smile and secretly promised Hari that he will also see if Hari could get a chance to work with Infosys. Hari gave him a tight hug and probably first time, he cried uncontrollably.

"Bye Riya, take care of yourself and Hari. And yes, make sure you don't forget me once I am out," he hugged her tightly and soon Riya burst into tears.

"Stop crying or else....", saying so, he himself started crying.

"Ok, I have got to go, else I will miss my flight," saying so he wiped off his tears from his right hand and sat in the cab. The cab soon left the place leaving behind a trail of smoke. But it also left a trail of memories for Hari and Riya.

ooo

It was two months since Rahul arrived in Bangalore with his mom and dad, but Shreya had met him hardly twice. Whenever he called her, she either ignored the calls or would tell an obvious lie that she is very busy. Though Rahul clearly understood each time she said a lie, he quietly ignored them hoping that some day she will be able to make her life stable.

It had been almost six months since he had come to Bangalore when he received a call from Riya. They hadn't talked ever since Rahul had left Gurgaon, and Rahul was happy to talk to her after such a long time.

"Hey dumbo, how are you? I heard you went to Bangalore. How is it going? You must be...." she continued ranting without waiting for a response.

"Hold madam, hold. Everything is good, in fact, fantastic. Why don't you come down too; we will have a blast," Rahul said, and he meant it genuinely.

"You have to sponsor my ticket in that case. Because as usual, I have spent all my salary on clothes. Heheh...." she giggled.

"Okay. I am sponsoring you. But you are coming to Bangalore this weekend. I won't listen to a no now."

"Okay. Done," Riya replied, reassuringly.

ooo

Rahul and Shreya were waiting at the airport for Riya. She had given them the flight number and the arrival time and it was almost time.

"Hey there ... look," Shreya shouted in Rahul's ears and pointed to the gate on the right hand side of the arrival terminal. Riya was coming, with just a bag in hand. They waved to her and she waved back.

They guided her to Rahul's car and drove back to Rahul's place where arrangements had been made for her stay. Riya knew Rahul's parents well and they did not have any problem with Riya staying there.

"You freshen up and have a good night's sleep. Because form tomorrow onwards, we are going to tire ourselves by having a blast," Rahul said and left her alone in the guestroom to change and freshen up.

The next day, it was a Sunday and they made a plan with Shreya to go to the malls, catch a movie and eat out.

"You ready dumbo?" Riya asked Rahul.

"Yup! Let's pick Shreya up and go," Rahul said excitedly. He was very happy to go on an outing with his best friend and the love of his life.

Shreya was already ready and was waiting impatiently for both of them to arrive. Her husband was still sleeping, as he usually did on most of the Sundays. The restrain in her relationship with her husband had pulled them a little apart. She didn't love her husband; but she cared for him. He was the only support system she had in the city.

Rahul parked the car in the visitor's parking, and both quickly jumped out to stop the lift. Both pressed the button at almost the same time. Pim Pom! As soon as the doors of the lift opened, Riya pushed Rahul aside and quickly went inside the lift. She started pressing the 5th floor button as many times as possible as if a child has got some toy to play with. The nerd person inside the lift quickly confined himself at one corner thinking Riya to be some abnormal kid.

Both reached at Shreya's door and Riya quickly started pressing the door bell. It was Shreya who opened the door and for next two minutes Rahul could just manage to smile while the two girls were busy hugging each other continuously.

"Ok girls, if you both are over with your '*Bharat-Milap*' we should get going now. We are already very late". He said interrupting both of them.

"Yes, we should," said Shreya and quickly went inside with a ruffle bag in her hand. "Nothing! Just had some home use stuff of a friend who left it at my place."

Everyone hopped inside the car quickly.

"So, where are we going first?" Shreya asked enthusiastically.

"We are going to the movie first, then we will have lunch and then we will go shopping. After that, we will have a late night coffee, go to a pub, dance and have a blast. After that...."

"Hold on Riya! How do you manage to speak so much," Shreya said, giggling. Rahul joined her in her giggles.

OOO

"Uff ... I am exhausted," Shreya remarked.

"I am not. Let's have a cup of coffee and then go to a pub," Riya said.

"Okay. I am game. What about you Shreya?" Rahul asked.

"I am game too."

"What about your husband? Ask him as well. He doesn't have a problem with this, does he?" Riya asked matter-of-factly.

Shreya gave her a nervous smile and didn't answer. Riya could sense something uneasy about the situation but decided not to prod further.

They drove the rest of the distance in silence and went to a coffee shop.

"What will you have dumbo?" Riya asked, breaking the silence with her effervescence.

"A cappuccino for me," he replied.

"A cappuccino for me too," Shreya butted in.

"Excuse me! Three cappuccino please! Thanks," Riya placed the order and the three of them took a corner table.

"So, how is Hari?" Rahul asked Riya.

"He is good," Riya replied and a shy smile broke across her face.

"Smiling! Hmm! Something going on between...." Shreya remarked, noticing the shy smile on her face.

"No, no … nothing like that. Oh, the coffee is here", Riya quickly changed the subject.

OOO

After having coffee, they decided to head back home. Rahul left a generous tip and walked towards the car, which was the only one standing outside.

"Hey Rahul. We need to give this bag to one of Riya's friends. Remind me when we reach near your place. Her home is near your place only," Shreya said as they were about to sit in the car.

"Okay"

○○○

"Hey, we are near my place. Who do you have to give that bag to?" Rahul asked, while he was about 2 minutes away from the place.

"Okay. Keep driving. I will tell you the way," Shreya said, and the two girls exchanged smiles.

"Okay."

"Hey, stop, stop, stop," Shreya shouted in front a large black gate.

"What? That's my place. You need to tell me...." Rahul said, perplexed.

Shreya interrupted him by handing him the bag. He understood it was meant for him and his joy knew no bounds. He opened it and found almost all the small home use stuff which he was planning to buy this weekend and had discussed with Shreya once. He felt like jumping onto the back seat and hugging her tightly. It felt like he had shared something passionate with her, like a kiss.

The two girls smiled on seeing his joy.

"Thanks," he stuttered with emotions while saying the word.

"Riya, you go upstairs. I will drop Shreya and come back," he said.

"Okay. Take her home safely, dumbo."

"Yeah, yeah."

ooo

The three of them went on another shopping trip the next day and then it was time for Riya to go back.

"I will miss you *yaar,*" Riya said, with tears in her eyes. She hugged both of them tightly.

"I will miss you too," Rahul said, gulping down his tears. "Keep in touch."

"I will remember this trip forever," Shreya said and hugged her again.

Riya's visit to Bangalore gave a new lease of life to the friendship between Rahul and Shreya. They continued to meet over the weekends. Rahul was enjoying his new job; just because of the fact that he was near the people he loved the most. It was the best time of his life. He was enjoying giving more of his time to Shreya. He was enjoying helping her out in the smallest of ways possible. Shreya was spending more time with him than her husband. But it didn't bother him. All he knew was he still loved her and would continue loving her for the rest of his life. And for the sake of her happiness, he could always be there to help her out in whatsoever way possible.

It was 11.30 a.m. Rahul was working on an important client deliverable. "Hello. Hey, what's up?" Rahul received a call from Shreya.

"Hey. Nothing much. I was just thinking if you could come down to this pub and we will have a blast. Some of my office friends are coming too. We will have fun," Shreya said.

"Okay. I will be at your place by 8:00 and we will go together."

"Cool."

She is introducing me to her friends for the first time. Wow. I know it's your game plan, he thought, and looked skywards.

He thought to finish the work earlier and leave. He enthusiastically finished his work by 4 o'clock. Here goes the final mail – he spoke to himself. Before leaving, he went to his Manager to inform that he has finished his set of work and has to leave early for some urgent work. Deep within his happiness knew no bounds, as it was almost 15-20 days since he had met Shreya.

"Hi Basu! I am leaving now for some personal work," Rahul quickly spoke to his Manager and thought to move back towards the door. "Ummm … Rahul! You know I see you as a matured person who is in a position to take my role. Why don't you complete the pending work of your peers, who are still struggling with there work," Basu responded with a cold face. 'Here goes today's program for a toss', Rahul thought in his mind almost cursing his Manager.

He remembered the words of his previous colleague who once said – "If you have a relationship, join this firm and your break up is guaranteed". It was only now when he was realising the true meanings of those words. He almost thumped his fist on the desk in anger which even sent a clear signal to others about his displeasure. Basu paused for a while, stared at Rahul clearly knowing his eagerness to leave, and got engrossed with his work as if he is completely unaware of his surroundings.

It was almost 7.30 when Shreya called her up – "Hey Rahul! When are you starting from your home?" 'How he can tell her that he is still in office', he thought to himself. He managed to quickly hide his anger against his Manager. "Hey Shreya! There is a huge traffic jam out here near my office. I am stuck there," he lied.

At 8 finally he managed to finish his work and was about to leave. He was about to shut down the PC when he received a ping by Basu – "I thought being a responsible member of the team, you would like to join the client call scheduled from 8 to 8.30." Almost out of his nerves, Rahul kept his calm and silently started dialling the conference bridge. At the same time, his cell phone started ringing with the screen showing 'Shreya Calling'. She was almost furious this time as her friends had already reached the pub. "Rahul! If you wish to come, come at the pub directly. I can't wait any longer. I am leaving," He quickly finished the client call and left without even caring a damn about his Manager now. He drove back home, half excited, half angry.

He entered his home and gave his mother, who was standing at the door, a peck on the cheek. He thumped his fist in the air and went straight to his room to quickly freshen up.

"Ma ... I am going out with a friend. Don't cook dinner for me," he shouted from his room itself.

He quickly opened his wardrobe and selected a navy blue coloured shirt. It was his favourite and he was confident Shreya would like it too. He then quickly dabbed on some after shave even though he had shaved in the morning. He changed into the navy blue shirt, put on a fitted pair of trousers and sprayed the most expensive perfume he had – which he had purchased from a flea market – on his body. Despite all his efforts, it was almost 9:00 by the time he got ready.

"Bye Ma. I am leaving. Will be late! You go to sleep. Good night", he said, and with hurried steps, went out of the house.

He reached the pub sharp at 9:30 p.m. Shreya was already standing at the door as he had messaged her 10 minutes before coming to her place. She was dressed in a red off shoulder top and matching skirt. The sight of her set Rahul's heart aflutter. She had done her hair in a different style, which gave him a sense of courting a *hoor* from heaven. The fact that he was not courting her didn't occur to him.

Every outing with her meant a date for him to understand her better. All he wanted was to make her life either stable or a chance to win her back.

"Hi! Why now? You should have come by 11.30 only when the pub will be closed! Now don't just stand like a fool and let's go," Shreya said taunting on him, and started walking inside the pub, without disturbing her elegant poise.

Rahul found it difficult to concentrate on his thoughts. Her smell, her sight and her aura pulled him and he glanced at her every now and then. They were at the most popular pub, Green Hazes, in the city. But it didn't matter to Rahul. He just wanted to be close to her, even if that meant going to a roadside stall.

They reached the table in the middle, which was already reserved for them. The pub had a typical ambience of a night club. Strobe lights were flashing all over, there was loud music playing and people could be seen talking in loud voices.

"Nice place," Rahul came close to Shreya's ear and shouted.

Shreya leaned forward and nodded in agreement.

"Hey, there they are," Shreya said and pointed towards the door. She waved the three figures standing at the door to catch their attention.

She had invited her colleagues Ravi and Vandana, who were a couple, as well as her VP, Sumit. The three of them made their way to the table.

"Rahul, this is Ravi and Vandana. Ravi and Vandana, this is Rahul, my friend," she introduced Rahul to the couple.

Rahul gave them a firm handshake and he shook hands with Sumit as well, before Shreya could introduce him.

"And he is our VP, Sumit," she said. And instantly, Rahul's grip weakened. He retracted and gave him a nervous smile.

Is it the same Sumit she told me about? Why has she invited him even after hearing such a lot about him? And why hasn't he brought his wife along? All kinds of questions reverberated in his mind. Shreya glanced towards Sumit several times and that further disturbed Rahul. He could see her obvious attraction for Sumit and it made her uncomfortable. Not only because he loved her, but because he could sense the intentions of Sumit and didn't want her to get hurt.

They took their seats and Shreya sat next to Sumit. It made Rahul more uncomfortable. They ordered their drinks, but Rahul was no longer interested in having fun. His evening was spoilt and all he wanted was to talk to Shreya alone and make her understand the implications of her actions. She regularly touched Sumit's hands during conversations and it sent a chill down Rahul's spine.

Rahul feared for her safety.

"Shreya, don't drink more. You have already had more than enough," he said, warning her.

"Nyah. I can still have more," Shreya replied, stuttering. Rahul tried to snatch Shreya's drink from her hand, but Sumit stopped him. "Let her drink man! After all why do we come to parties? To enjoy, to have fun!"

All of them sat at the pub for close to two hours, after which, they decided to call it quits. Shreya had had the maximum number of shots and was beginning to feel the heat. She kept her head on Sumit's shoulders and asked him for his support.

Rahul felt helpless. He wished he could shout out loud and ask her to stay away from that unscrupulous man but knew Shreya would take it otherwise. He offered a hand to Shreya but Sumit had already picked her up and had started walking towards the car. Shreya held on to Sumit like a new born child, afraid of falling down.

"I can't go home in this condition. My husband would kill me," Shreya said, half conscious of her words.

"She can stay at my place," Rahul butted in quickly, before Sumit could say a word. He could sense the lust in his eyes and didn't want Shreya to be the victim.

They put Shreya on the back seat of the car and Sumit sat alongside her, against Rahul's unvocal wishes.

"Rahul, right?" Sumit asked him in a condescending tone.

"Yup," he replied, arrogantly.

"Drop me and Shreya to my place first. I will tell you the way."

He didn't respond and turned the key in the ignition.

He followed Sumit's instructions until they reached his home.

"Thanks mate," Sumit said. "Come Shreya. Let's go. You can stay at my place," he said to Shreya, who was sitting erect on the back seat of the car.

"Shreya is going to my place. It's okay. I can keep her," Rahul retorted, almost at the point of yelling.

"Who are you to decide?" Shreya said, irritated, and got down.

Sumit helped her along to the door, and Rahul just kept waiting. He felt like grabbing her and forcing her to come to his place, but knew it wouldn't solve the purpose. He desperately wanted to help her, but knew she didn't want his help. He was feeling completely helpless now.

Tears almost came to the cores of his eyes and he decided to head back home and never talk to her again. He reached home around 1 o'clock. His mother was waiting for him eagerly.

"Finally, you are home. You had dinner na?" his mother asked.

She didn't get a response. Rahul went to his room and shut the door without talking to his mother. The flood of tears started flowing down his eyes. He imagined about Shreya and cursed himself for his helplessness. 'Had I shown a little more courage, I could have taken her away from the clutches of that bastard Sumit', he was thinking while trying hard to sleep. But sleep was miles away from him today.

ooo

He was feeling alone again without Shreya. The same job which gave him immense happiness till a month back now irritated him. It had almost a month since the pub incident and he hadn't talked to her since. He called her a couple of times, but she ignored his calls. He wanted somebody to listen to his feelings, and decided to give Hari a call. He hadn't called him ever since he left Gurgaon.

"Hi Hari. What's up bro?" he said, as Hari picked up the call. He tried to sound as cheerful as possible.

"Everything fantastic. You tell me. How is your new job going on? And how is Shreya?" Hari asked, cheerfully, happy to hear from him.

But he had accidentally broached the topic Rahul was avoiding. Emotions flooded inside Rahul and he could no longer hold back his tears. He told Hari everything about the pub incident.

"Could you please tell her that Sumit is not the right kind of guy? Could you please tell her that all I want is her to be safe? Please," he choked.

"Sure. I will do that. You don't worry. She would talk to you. You are her best friend. Always remember that", Hari consoled him, and held back his own tears.

OOO

Time went by and it was a week since Rahul had a chat with Hari. He was feeling uneasy and wanted someone to talk to. He could think of nobody other than Shreya. He decided to call her but his calls went unanswered repeatedly. Almost losing his composure, he thought of dialling one last time.

'I will not call her ever if she doesn't pick up the call', Rahul said to himself.

"Hi Shreya, Rahul here," he spoke when Shreya answered the call. He quickly forgot all the bitterness. He forgot all what he thought to say to Shreya.

"Would you stop calling me for God's sake? Let me live my life, please," she yelled at him without even listening to him. "You have always taken things for granted. You are not my husband, but you always make me feel guilty about things. It's up to me who I want to go home with. Who are you to interfere in that? When my husband doesn't have a problem, why do you have a problem? It's you who is complicating my life and not Sumit. My life would have been much simpler had you not been there in my life," she said.

Rahul kept the phone down without saying a word. *Had you not been there in my life ....* The words pricked at his skin like a three-pronged fork. He decided he would make life simpler for her.

He started his car, without knowing where he was heading. At one point, he decided to go to Shreya's place and tell her how much he loved her, and all he wanted was her safety. But he decided against it.

He didn't have any control over the car, and the car of his emotions. He never realised he was pushing the paddle too much and that the car was going at a very fast speed. He couldn't see the road ahead. All he could see was the pub, drunk Shreya and Sumit taking her in her arms. The scene blurred his vision. *Had you not been there in my life ....* The words came back to him. And then, there was a loud thud ... and silence....

The Grief

Shreya paced up and down, looking at the clock repeatedly. It was 12 p.m. and her husband had not yet come home. He normally came home by 7, except on the days when there was an important meeting in the office. Something pulled at her heart. She had a foreboding feeling about it, which she tried to resist by walking at a quick pace.

The darkness outside was customary for that hour, but it gave her a sense of darkness taking control of her life. She had never felt that way before and it made her feel nervous. She tried calling his cell phone but it was out of reach. She repeatedly called it every 10 minutes, until she was finally exhausted and settled down in a chair.

Her bodily reactions prompted her eyelids to close but the fear in her would not let her sleep. She sat in the chair staring at the clock, until she didn't know where she was.

Tuk tuk tuk .... Shreya got up with a jerk. She looked to her right and then quickly to her left. It took her a while to judge that it was a chair she was sitting in, and then, the happenings of the night gone by flashed in front of her ... she remembered her husband, his not coming home, her waiting in anxiety and then her going off to sleep finally.

Tuk tuk tuk .... there was another knock on the door, a louder one. She expected it to be her husband and toughened up to teach him a lesson for getting her so worried. She ruffled her hair to set them in order and with a strict gait walked towards the door. She wanted to be strict, but the same uneasiness of the previous night pulled at her as she approached the door; and finally, it gave away as the door opened.

A few men stood at the door, in tattered clothes. They looked as if they hadn't taken a bath since ages. But Shreya didn't notice any of that. Her gaze went straight to the mass wrapped in white cloth in their hands which they were holding onerously. And she didn't realise what hit her.

The bruised face peeking out of white cloth wrapped tightly around that dead mass was familiar to her. It was her husband.

Her reactions were numbed. She didn't say a word and involuntarily widened the door for the men to come in and keep the body. She kept staring at them while they kept the body in the centre of her drawing room.

"Madam, everything will be alright," a man came close to her and tried to give her solace. She couldn't hear a word.

"A car hit him. We were working nearby. He was hit badly," another one of the men said, in broken English and continued, "we took him to the hospital in an auto rickshaw, but he was already dead. The doctor found out his wallet from his jeans which had the address of here."

She didn't look at him as he spoke. It was as though he was speaking some foreign language that was incomprehensible to her. She quietly gazed at the body lying in front of her and wondered when it might jump at her. It didn't.

"We noted the car number which hit him. He was driving at a very fast speed. Here, this is the car's number," a man in a vest

and a thin cloth wrapped around his legs spoke and gave her a white chit which had some digits and alphabets written on it.

BN 01 F 5678. It was gibberish to her. She couldn't comprehend the shape and the structure of the writing on the paper. The men quietly went away, without saying another word. And she was left all to herself, except the white chit of paper and her husband's body. She stared at the paper in her left hand again to make sense of what was happening.

And a feeling of outrageousness ran through her. Her subconscious mind told her it was a number she had come across and then it dawned on her – it was the number of Rahul's car. Her grief turned into extreme anger and without a second thought, she got up, took the car keys hanging near the entrance as usual and stomped towards her car. She forgot about her husband's body lying inside the house; she forgot she had to call up her and her husband's family to inform them about the incident; she forgot everything about her social obligations and duties. All she wanted was revenge for the act and harming Rahul was the only plausible way she could think of.

She didn't feel any emotions inside her, except that of anger and betrayal. Her soul didn't say a word, as if it has vanished altogether. She drove the car at a breakneck speed, without paying any heed to the traffic rules. It was six in the morning and there wasn't much traffic around.

Hardly putting the foot on the brake, she honked the way through the streets. The car was going at full throttle, and something strange happened all of a sudden.

While driving she heard someone calling out her name, so slowly as if it's coming from the far end of a dark tunnel. She looked around to find out the person but all she could see in front was heavy fog. It seemed as if someone is slowly taking control over her and trying to invade her thoughts....

She came back to her senses, and was sweating profusely. Her heartbeat was racing all the way. Before she could even realise or think about this strange incident, angrily she came to a complete halt in front of a large black gate, which was wide open. There were poles dug by the side of the gate and a white canopy was mounted on top of the poles. There was a crowd outside the house, all with mellow expression on their faces. But none of it hit her senses. She could not see any of it – neither the white canopy, nor the uneasy silence of the place.

Her anger didn't let her see anything. She barged inside the house, pushing aside people forcefully and spoke with full force, for the first time since the night before, "Where is Rahul?" the tone of her pitch reaching the maximum. Her shriek cut through the silence like a sword.

She didn't realise she was standing in the middle of the drawing room in Rahul's house, and there was a mass wrapped in white cloth, like the one back at her home, near her feet.

She looked to her right and she saw a familiar figure, who had just turned around at her shriek. Before she could say another word, the familiar figure clutched her left arm and gave her a jolt. It was Hari.

"What have you come here for now?" Hari said, with a frown of his eyebrows. "How the hell did you have the courage to come to this place?" he continued, his voice rising with every sentence.

"Just get lost before I do anything to you," Hari warned her, without keeping any of his anger hidden. Hari's rough tone woke her up and she became aware of her surroundings. She noticed the crowd of people, the sombre atmosphere and the uneasy silence of the place.

She broke into tears. "Where is Rahul?" she asked him, crying, because she already knew the answer by then. And then she looked down at the body near her feet which was wrapped in white cloth and fell to her knees. She could see the bruised face of the body now. It was the same face which had helped her so many times in her life; it was the face which was always there for her when she was in trouble; it was the face which once sat next to her in office; it was Rahul.

But before she could feel her grief, Hari grabbed her by her arm and took her outside.

"You are the reason for all of this. It would never have happened had you...." he paused, holding back his anger. She kept crying, without asking for any explanation.

"You know he called me the last day and that bastard was still saying" ... Hari paused for a while and tried to wipe off the tears which were all set to flood out. He somehow composed himself back and continued – "Sorry not the bastard but that bloody emotional fool still just wanted nothing for himself, but a stable and happy life for you."

He paused for a while and looked at the sun which had started rising by now. But deep inside Hari knew that his brightest sun had already set and will never ever rise again. Tears once again were ready to jump out from his eyes. He continued – "You will never be able to understand the difference between the face value and the hidden intentions of the people like Sumit. You always liked spending time with good-looking guys, and never ever understood whether they are interested in you as a person or just want physical pleasures from you. You never valued love. When it came, you still closed your eyes. God damn it, you know Rahul actually died the same day when you went out with Sumit, got drunk and stayed back at his place. I don't know if your husband knows all this but I am definitely going to tell him," Hari continued speaking at a fast clip without waiting for any kind of response.

The last sentence hit her like a nail. She vividly remembered her husband's body lying in her house; but she chose to stay mum.

"Had you only respected his feelings, the soft feelings which got crushed unknowingly, several times, Rahul would have been alive by now. You will never understand the meaning of love because you never understood how much he loved you. Now don't stand here shamelessly and go back wherever you wish to, no one is ever going to stop you now. I just wish that you long for the same care and love which you have always ignored."

Hari could not stop his emotions and quickly went inside, leaving her all alone in the crowd of people. She kept looking at the sky, and two drops of tears silently came out from her eyes.

Epilogue

She took the bottle lying in her kitchen and popped a few pills out of it on her hands. She looked intently at them, while her hands shook. She had a glass of water in one hand and the pills in another, but she could not bring her hand close to her mouth to swallow them. Shreya didn't have the courage to end her life.

She dropped the pills and the glass of water and ran outside. She desperately wanted someone to listen to her agony, her pain, but there was nobody around. She tried to take solace in the setting sun and the dark clouds. Suddenly, it started raining.

A few rain drops fell on her eyes, which were wet already. And soon, the drizzle turned into a torrential rain. It was only the second time she had seen such rain. Her mind went some years ago when she had experienced such rain for the first time; and words echoed in her subconscious- "Today, I want to talk to you and you don't have time. Tomorrow, you would want to talk to me and I won't be around." These were Rahul's words and they came to haunt her back.

She looked skywards. Somewhere in the clouds, she could still sense Rahul standing, worried over her pain and agony and desperately trying to get in touch with her; but was unable to do so. She wished the dark clouds could stay there forever;

she wished Rahul would someday come out of those clouds and say, "Let me know if …" the same way he used to say in the first line of the SMS after she didn't answer his calls.

She wished she could have done things differently. She wished she could take time backwards and make amends for whatever she had done wrong. And then, her train of thoughts was broken.

She saw a boy, around five years old, standing at the gate, with an umbrella in his hand. The innocence on his face made her smile. And then her eyes went to the two figures standing behind the boy. It was Hari and Riya.

"Hi Shreya, how are you?" Hari said.

"Fine," Shreya replied, not knowing how to react seeing them after such a long time.

"He's our son," Riya replied, as if she read the puzzled expression on her face.

"That's....great. Congrats. He looks like a lovely boy," Shreya replied, smiling nervously.

"What's your name honey?" Shreya said, extending her arm for a handshake.

With the same familiar smile and innocence, the boy replied, "Rahul."